DEEP TROUBLE

GOOSEBUMPS®

Also available as ebooks

ALSO AVAILABLE:

Goosebumps®

DEEP TROUBLE

R.L. STINE

SCHOLASTIC INC.

NEW YORK TORONTO LONDON AUCKLAND SYDNEY
MEXICO CITY NEW DELHI HONG KONG BUENOS AIRES

No part of this publication may be reproduced, stored in a retrieval system, or transmitted in any form or by any means, electronic, mechanical, photocopying, recording, or otherwise, without written permission of the publisher. For information regarding permission, write to Scholastic Inc., Attention: Permissions Department, 557 Broadway, New York, NY 10012.

ISBN: 978-1-76015-994-8

Goosebumps book series created by Parachute Press, Inc.

Copyright © 1994 by Scholastic Inc.

All rights reserved. Published by Scholastic Inc., *Publishers since 1920*. SCHOLASTIC, GOOSEBUMPS, GOOSEBUMPS HORRORLAND and associated logos are trademarks and/or registered trademarks of Scholastic Inc.

This edition published in 2015 by Scholastic Australia.

10 9 8 7 6 5 4 3 2   15 16 17 18 19 / 1

Printed by McPherson's Printing Group, Maryborough, VIC.

"Behind the Screams" bonus material by Matthew D. Payne

MIX
Paper from
responsible sources
FSC® C001695

1

There I was, two hundred feet under the sea.

I was on the hunt of my life. The hunt for the Great White Stingray.

That's what they called him at Coast Guard headquarters. But me, I called him Joe.

The giant stingray had already stung ten swimmers. People were afraid to step into the water. Panic spread all up and down the coast.

That's why they sent for me.

William Deep, Jr., of Baltimore, Maryland.

Yes, William Deep, Jr., world-famous twelve-year-old undersea explorer. Solver of scary ocean problems.

I captured the Great White Shark that terrorized Myrtle Beach. I proved he wasn't so great!

I fought the giant octopus that ate the entire California Championship Surfing Team.

I unplugged the electric eel that sent shock waves all over Miami.

But now I faced the fight of my life. Joe, the Great White Stingray.

Somewhere down deep under the sea, he lurked.

I had everything I needed: scuba suit, flippers, mask, oxygen tank, and poison-dart gun.

Wait — did something move? Just behind that giant clam?

I raised my dart gun and waited for an attack.

Then, suddenly, my mask clouded. I couldn't breathe.

I strained for breath. No air came.

My oxygen tank! Someone must have tampered with it!

There was no time to lose. Two hundred feet down — and no air! I had to surface — fast!

I kicked my legs, desperately trying to pull myself to the surface.

Holding my breath. My lungs about to burst. I was losing strength, getting dizzy.

Would I make it? Or would I die right here, deep under the ocean, Joe the Stingray's dinner?

Panic swept over me like an ocean tide. I searched through the fogged mask for my diving partner. Where was she when I needed her?

Finally, I spotted her swimming up at the surface, near the boat.

Help me! Save me! No air! I tried to tell her, waving my arms like a maniac.

Finally, she noticed me. She swam toward me and dragged my dazed and limp body to the surface.

I ripped off my mask and sucked in mouthfuls of air.

"What's your problem, Aqua Man?" she cried. "Did a jellyfish sting you?"

My diving partner is very brave. She laughs in the face of danger.

I struggled to catch my breath. "No air. Someone — cut off — tank —"

Then everything went black.

My diving partner shoved my head back under the water. I opened my eyes and came up sputtering.

"Get real, Billy," she said. "Can't you snorkel without acting like a total jerk?"

I sighed. She was no fun.

My "diving partner" was really just my bratty sister, Sheena. I was only pretending to be William Deep, Jr., undersea explorer.

But would it kill Sheena to go along with it just once?

My name actually *is* William Deep, Jr., but everybody calls me Billy. I'm twelve — I think I mentioned that already.

Sheena is ten. She looks like me. We both have straight black hair, but mine is short and hers goes down to her shoulders. We're both skinny, with knobby knees and elbows, and long, narrow feet. We both have dark blue eyes and thick, dark eyebrows.

Other than that, we're not alike at all.

Sheena has no imagination. She was never afraid of monsters in her closet when she was little. She didn't believe in Santa Claus or the tooth fairy, either. She loves to say, "There's no such thing."

I dove underwater and pinched Sheena's leg. *Attack of the Giant Lobster Man!*

"Stop it!" she screamed. She kicked me in the shoulder. I came up for air.

"Hey, you two," my uncle said. "Be careful down there."

My uncle stood on the deck of his sea lab boat, the *Cassandra*. He peered down at Sheena and me snorkeling nearby.

My uncle's name is George Deep, but everybody calls him Dr. D. Even my dad, who is his brother, calls him Dr. D. Maybe that's because he looks just the way a scientist should.

Dr. D is short, thin, wears glasses and a very serious, thoughtful expression. He has curly brown hair and a bald spot at the back of his head. Anyone who saw him would say, "I bet you're a scientist."

Sheena and I were visiting Dr. D on the *Cassandra*. Every year our parents let us spend our summer vacation with Dr. D. It sure beats hanging out at home. This summer, we were anchored just off a tiny island called Ilandra, in the Caribbean Sea.

Dr. D is a marine biologist. He specializes in tropical marine life. He studies the habits of tropical fish and looks for new kinds of ocean plants and fish that haven't been discovered yet

The *Cassandra* is a big and sturdy boat. It is about fifty feet long. Dr. D uses most of the space for labs and research rooms. Up on deck is a cockpit, where he steers the boat. He keeps a dinghy tied to the starboard, or right side of the deck, and a huge glass tank on the port, or left side.

Sometimes Dr. D catches very big fish and keeps them temporarily in the glass tank — usually just long enough to tag the fish for research, or care for them if they are sick or injured.

The rest of the deck is open space, good for playing catch or sunbathing.

Dr. D's research takes him all over the world. He isn't married and doesn't have any kids. He says he's too busy staring at fish.

But he likes kids. That's why he invites me and Sheena to visit him every summer.

"Stick close together, kids," Dr. D said. "And don't swim off too far. Especially you, Billy."

He narrowed his eyes at me. That's his "I mean it" look. He never narrows his eyes at Sheena.

"There've been reports of some shark sightings in the area," he said.

"Sharks! Wow!" I cried.

Dr. D frowned at me. "Billy," he said. "This is serious. Don't leave the boat. And don't go near the reef."

I knew he was going to say that.

Clamshell Reef is a long red coral reef just a few hundred yards away from where we were anchored. I'd been dying to explore it ever since we got there.

"Don't worry about me, Dr. D," I called up to him. "I won't get into trouble."

Sheena muttered under her breath, "Yeah, right."

I reached out to give her another lobster pinch, but she dove underwater.

"Good," said Dr. D. "Now don't forget — if you see a shark fin, try not to splash around a lot. Movement will attract it. Just slowly, steadily return to the boat."

"We won't forget," said Sheena, who had come up behind me, splashing like crazy.

I couldn't help feeling just a little bit excited. I'd always wanted to see a real, live shark.

I'd seen sharks at the aquarium, of course. But they were trapped in a glass tank, where they just swam around restlessly, perfectly harmless.

Not very exciting.

I wanted to spot a shark's fin on the horizon, floating over the water, closer, closer, heading right for us. . . .

In other words, I wanted adventure.

7

The *Cassandra* was anchored out in the ocean, a few hundred yards away from Clamshell Reef. The reef surrounded the island. Between the reef and the island stretched a beautiful lagoon.

Nothing was going to stop me from exploring that lagoon — no matter what Dr. D said.

"Come on, Billy," Sheena called, adjusting her mask. "Let's check out that school of fish."

She pointed to a patch of tiny ripples in the water near the bow of the boat. She slid the mouthpiece into her mouth and lowered her head into the water. I followed her to the ripples.

Soon Sheena and I were surrounded by hundreds of tiny neon-blue fish.

Underwater, I always felt as if I were in a faraway world. *Breathing through the snorkel, I could live down here with the fish and the dolphins*, I thought. *After a while, maybe I would grow flippers and a fin.*

The tiny blue fish began to swim away, and I swam with them. They were so great-looking! I didn't want them to leave me behind.

Suddenly, the fish all darted from view. I tried to follow, but they were too fast.

They had vanished!

Had something scared them away?

I glanced around. Clumps of seaweed floated near the surface. Then I saw a flash of red.

I floated closer, peering through the mask. A few yards ahead of me I saw bumpy red formations. Red coral.

Oh, no, I thought. *Clamshell Reef. Dr. D told me not to swim this far.*

I began to turn around. I knew I should swim back to the boat.

But I was tempted to stay and explore a little. After all, I was already there.

The reef looked like a red sand castle, filled with underwater caves and tunnels. Small fish darted in and out of them. The fish were bright yellow and blue.

Maybe I could swim over and explore one of those tunnels, I thought. *How dangerous could it be?*

Suddenly, I felt something brush against my leg. It tickled and sent a tingle up my leg.

A fish?

I glanced around, but I didn't see anything.

Then I felt it again.

A tingling against my leg.

And then it clutched me.

Again I turned to see what it was. Again I saw nothing.

My heart began to race. I knew it was probably nothing dangerous. But I wished I could see it.

I turned and started back for the boat, kicking hard.

But something grabbed my right leg — and held on!

I froze in fear. Then I frantically kicked my leg as hard as I could.

Let go! Let go of me!

I couldn't see it — and I couldn't pull free!

The water churned and tossed as I kicked with all my strength.

Overcome with terror, I lifted my head out of the water and choked out a weak cry: "Help!"

But it was no use.

Whatever it was, it kept pulling me down. Down.

Down to the bottom of the sea.

"Help!" I cried out again. "Sheena! Dr. D!"

I was dragged below the surface again. I felt the slimy tentacle tighten around my ankle.

As I sank underwater, I turned — and saw it.

It loomed huge and dark.

A sea monster!

Through the churning waters, it glared at me with one giant brown eye. The terrifying creature floated underwater like an enormous dark green balloon. Its mouth opened in a silent cry, revealing two rows of jagged, sharp teeth.

An enormous octopus! But it had at least *twelve* tentacles!

Twelve long, slimy tentacles. One was wrapped around my ankle. Another one slid toward me.

NO!

My arms thrashed in the water.

I gulped in mouthfuls of air.

I struggled to the surface — but the huge creature dragged me down again.

I couldn't believe it. As I sank, scenes from my life actually flashed before my eyes.

I saw my parents, waving to me as I boarded the yellow school bus for my first day of school.

Mom and Dad! I'll never see them again!

What a way to go, I thought. *Killed by a sea monster!*

No one will believe it.

Everything started to turn red. I felt dizzy, weak.

But something was pulling me, pulling me up.

Up to the surface. Away from the tentacled monster.

I opened my eyes, choking and sputtering.

I stared up at Dr. D!

"Billy! Are you all right?" Dr. D studied me with concern.

I coughed and nodded. I kicked my right leg. The slimy tentacle was gone.

The dark creature had vanished.

"I heard you screaming and saw you thrashing about," said Dr. D. "I swam over from the boat as fast as I could. What happened?"

Dr. D had a yellow life jacket over his shoulders. He slipped a rubber lifesaver right over my head. I floated easily now, the life ring under my arms.

I had lost my flippers in the struggle. My mask and snorkle dangled around my neck.

Sheena swam over and floated beside me, treading water.

"It grabbed my leg!" I cried breathlessly. "It tried to pull me under!"

"What grabbed your leg, Billy?" asked Dr. D. "I don't see anything around here —"

"It was a sea monster," I told him. "A huge one! I felt its slimy tentacle grabbing my leg....*Ouch!*"

Something pinched my toe.

"It's back!" I shrieked in horror.

Sheena popped out of the water and shook her wet hair, laughing.

"That was me, you dork!" she cried.

"Billy, Billy," Dr. D murmured. "You and your wild imagination." He shook his head. "You nearly scared me to death. Please — don't ever do that again. Your leg probably got tangled in a piece of seaweed, that's all."

"But — but — !" I sputtered.

He dipped his hand in the water and pulled up a handful of slimy green strings. "There's seaweed everywhere.

"But I saw it!" I shouted. "I saw its tentacles, its big pointy teeth!"

"There's no such thing as sea monsters," said Sheena. Miss Know-It-All.

"Let's discuss it on the boat," my uncle said, dropping the clump of seaweed back in the water.

"Come on. Swim back with me. And stay away from the reef. Swim around it."

He turned around and started swimming toward the *Cassandra*." I saw that the sea monster had pulled me into the lagoon. The reef lay between us and the boat. But there was a break in the reef we could swim through.

I followed them, thinking angry thoughts.

Why didn't they believe me?

I had seen the creature grab my leg. It wasn't a stupid clump of seaweed. It wasn't my imagination.

I was determined to prove them wrong. I'd find that creature and show it to them myself — someday. But not today.

Now I was ready to get back to the safety of the boat.

I swam up to Sheena and called, "Race you to the boat."

"Last one there is a chocolate-covered jelly-fish!" she cried.

Sheena can't refuse a race. She started speeding toward the boat, but I caught her by the arm.

"Wait," I said. "No fair. You're wearing flippers. Take them off."

"Too bad!" she cried, and pulled away. "See you at the boat!" I watched her splash away, building up a good lead.

She's not going to win, I decided.

I stared at the reef up ahead.

It would be faster just to swim over the reef. A shortcut.

I turned and started to swim straight toward the red coral.

"Billy! Get back here!" Dr. D shouted.

I pretended I didn't hear him.

The reef loomed ahead. I was almost there.

I saw Sheena splashing ahead of me. I kicked extra hard. I knew she'd never have the guts to swim over the reef. She'd swim around the end of it. I would cut through and beat her.

But my arms suddenly began to ache. I wasn't used to swimming so far.

Maybe I can stop at the reef and rest my arms for a second, I thought.

I reached the reef. I turned around. Sheena was swimming to the left, around the reef. I figured I had a few seconds to rest.

I stepped onto the red coral reef —

— and screamed in horror!

My foot burned as if it were on fire. The throbbing pain shot up my leg.

I screamed and dove into the water.

When I surfaced, I heard Sheena yelling, "Dr. D! Come quick!"

My foot burned, even in the cold ocean water.

Dr. D came up beside me. "Billy, what's the problem now?" he demanded.

"I saw him do something really stupid," Sheena said, smirking.

If my foot hadn't been burning up, I definitely would have punched out her lights.

"My foot!" I moaned. "I stepped on the reef — and — and —"

Dr. D held on to the lifesaver ring around my waist. "Ow. That's painful," he said, reaching up to pat my shoulder. "But you'll be all right. The burning will stop in a little while."

He pointed to the reef. "All that bright red coral is fire coral."

"Huh? Fire coral?" I stared back at it.

"Even I knew that!" Sheena said.

"It's covered with a mild poison," my uncle continued. "When it touches your skin, it burns like fire."

Now *he tells me*, I thought.

"Don't you know *anything*?" Sheena asked sarcastically.

She was asking for it. She really was.

"You're lucky you only burned your foot," Dr. D said. "Coral can be very sharp. You could have cut your foot and gotten poison into your bloodstream. Then you'd *really* be in trouble."

"Wow! What kind of trouble?" Sheena asked. She seemed awfully eager to hear about all the terrible things that could have happened to me.

Dr. D's expression turned serious. "The poison could paralyze you," he said.

"Oh, great," I said.

"So keep away from the red coral from now on," Dr. D warned. "And stay away from the lagoon, too."

"But that's where the sea monster lives!" I protested. "We have to go back there. I have to show it to you!"

Sheena bobbed in the blue-green water. "No such thing, no such thing," she chanted. Her favorite phrase. "No such thing — right, Dr. D?"

"Well, you never know," Dr. D replied thoughtfully. "We don't know all of the creatures that live in the oceans, Sheena. It's better to say that scientists have never seen one."

"So there, She-Ra," I said.

Sheena spit a stream of water at me. She hates it when I call her She-Ra.

"Listen, kids — I'm serious about staying away from this area," said Dr. D. "There may not be a sea monster in that lagoon, but there could be sharks, poisonous fish, electric eels. Any number of dangerous creatures. Don't swim over there."

He paused and frowned at me, as if to make sure I'd been paying attention.

"How's your foot feeling, Billy?" he asked.

"It's a little better now," I told him.

"Good. Enough adventure for one morning. Let's get back to the boat. It's almost lunchtime."

We all started swimming back to the *Cassandra*.

As I kicked, I felt something tickle my leg again.

Seaweed?

No.

It brushed against my thigh like — *fingers*.

"Cut it out, Sheena," I shouted angrily. I spun around to splash water in her face.

But she wasn't there. She wasn't anywhere near me.

She was up ahead, swimming beside Dr. D.

Sheena couldn't possibly have tickled me.

But something definitely *did*.

I stared down at the water, suddenly gripped with terror.

What was down there?

Why was it teasing me like that?

Was it preparing to grab me again and pull me down forever?

Alexander DuBrow, Dr. D's assistant, helped us aboard the boat.

"Hey, I heard shouting," Alexander said. "Is everything okay?"

"Everything is fine, Alexander," said Dr. D. "Billy stepped on some fire coral, but he's all right."

As I climbed up the ladder, Alexander grabbed my hands and pulled me aboard.

"Wow, Billy," he said. "Fire coral. I accidentally bumped into the fire coral my first day here. I saw stars. I really did, man. You sure you're okay?"

I nodded and showed him my foot. "It feels better now. But that wasn't the worst thing that happened. I was almost eaten by a sea monster!"

"No such thing, no such thing," Sheena chanted.

"I really saw it," I insisted. "They don't believe

me. But it was there. In the lagoon. It was big and green and —"

Alexander smiled. "If you say so, Billy," he said. He winked at Sheena.

I wanted to punch out his lights, too.

Big deal science student. What did *he* know?

Alexander was in his early twenties. But, unlike Dr. D, he didn't look like a scientist.

He looked more like a football player. He was very tall, about six feet four inches, and muscular. He had thick, wavy blond hair and blue eyes that crinkled in the corners. He had broad shoulders and big powerful-looking hands. He spent a lot of time in the sun and had a smooth, dark tan.

"I hope you're all hungry," Alexander said. "I made chicken salad sandwiches for lunch."

"Oh. Great," Sheena said, rolling her eyes.

Alexander did most of the cooking. He thought he was good at it. But he wasn't.

I went belowdecks to my cabin to change out of my wet bathing suit. My cabin was really just a tiny sleeping cubby with a cupboard for my things. Sheena had one just like it. Dr. D and Alexander had bigger cabins that they could actually walk around in.

We ate in the galley, which was what Dr. D called the boat's kitchen. It had a built-in table and built-in seats, and a small area for cooking.

When I entered the galley, Sheena was already sitting at the table. There was a big sandwich on a plate in front of her and one waiting for me.

Neither of us was too eager to try Alexander's chicken salad. The night before, we had eaten brussels sprouts casserole. For breakfast this morning, he served us whole wheat pancakes that sank to the bottom of my stomach like the *Titanic* going down!

"You first," I whispered to my sister.

"Uh-uh," Sheena said, shaking her head. "You try it. You're older."

My stomach growled. I sighed. There was nothing to do but taste it.

I sank my teeth into the sandwich and started chewing.

Not bad, I thought at first. A little chicken, a little mayonnaise. It actually tasted like a regular chicken salad sandwich.

Then, suddenly, my tongue started to burn. My whole mouth was on fire!

I let out a cry and grabbed for the glass of iced tea in front of me. I downed the entire glass.

"Fire coral!" I screamed. "You put fire coral in the chicken salad!"

Alexander laughed. "Just a little chili pepper. For taste. You like it?"

"I think I'd rather have cereal for lunch," Sheena said, setting down her sandwich. "If you don't mind."

"You can't have cereal for every meal," Alexander replied, frowning. "No wonder you're so skinny, Sheena. You never eat anything but cereal. Where's your spirit of adventure?"

"I think I'll have cereal, too," I said sheepishly. "Just for a change of pace."

Dr. D came into the galley. "What's for lunch?" he asked.

"Chicken salad sandwiches," said Alexander. "I made them spicy."

"*Very* spicy," I warned him.

Dr. D glanced at me and raised an eyebrow. "Oh, really?" he said. "You know, I'm not very hungry. I think I'll just have cereal for lunch."

"Maybe Billy and I could make dinner tonight," Sheena offered. She poured cereal into a bowl and added milk. "It's not fair for Alexander to cook *all* the time."

"That's a nice idea, Sheena," said Dr. D. "What do you two know how to make?"

"I know how to make brownies from a mix," I offered.

"And I know how to make fudge," said Sheena.

"Hmm," said Dr. D. "Maybe *I'll* cook tonight. How does grilled fish sound?"

"Great!" I said.

* * *

23

After lunch, Dr. D went into his office to go over some notes. Alexander led Sheena and me into the main lab to show us around.

The work lab was really cool. It had three big glass tanks along the wall filled with weird, amazing fish.

The smallest tank held two bright yellow sea horses and an underwater trumpet. The underwater trumpet was a long red-and-white fish shaped like a tube. There were also a lot of guppies swimming around in this tank.

Another tank held some flame angelfish, which were orange-red like fire, and a harlequin tuskfish with orange and aqua tiger stripes for camouflage.

The biggest tank held a long black-and-yellow snakelike thing with a mouth full of teeth.

"Ugh!" Sheena made a disgusted face as she stared at the long fish. "That one is really gross!"

"That's a black ribbon eel," said Alexander. "He bites, but he's not deadly. We call him Biff."

I snarled through the glass at Biff, but he ignored me.

I wondered what it would be like to come face-to-face with Biff in the ocean. His teeth looked nasty, but he wasn't nearly as big as the sea monster. I figured William Deep, Jr., world-famous undersea explorer, could handle it.

I turned away from the fish tanks and stood by the control panel, staring at all the knobs and dials.

"What does this do?" I asked. I pushed a button. A loud horn blared. We all jumped, startled.

"It honks the horn," Alexander said, laughing.

"Dr. D told Billy not to touch things without asking first," said Sheena. "He's told him a million times. He never listens."

"Shut up, She-Ra!" I said sharply.

"*You* shut up."

"Hey — no problem," said Alexander, raising both hands, motioning for us to chill out. "No harm done."

I turned back to the panel. Most of the dials were lit up, with little red indicators moving across their faces. I noticed one dial that was dark, its red indicator still.

"What's this for?" I asked, pointing to the dark dial. "It looks like you forgot to turn it on."

"Oh, that controls the Nansen bottle," Alexander said. "It's broken."

"What's a Nansen bottle?" asked Sheena.

"It collects samples of seawater from way down deep," said Alexander.

"Why don't you fix it?" I asked.

"We can't afford to," said Alexander.

"Why not?" asked Sheena. "Doesn't the university give you money?"

We both knew that Dr. D's research was paid for by a university in Ohio.

"They gave us money for our research," Alexander explained. "But it's almost gone. We're waiting to see if they'll give us more. In the meantime, we don't have the money to fix things."

"What if the *Cassandra* breaks down or something?" I asked.

"Then I guess we'll have to put her in dry dock for a while," said Alexander. "Or else find a new way to get more money."

"Wow," said Sheena. "That would mean no more summer visits."

I hated to think of the *Cassandra* just sitting on a dock. Even worse was the thought of Dr. D being stuck on land with no fish to study.

Our uncle was miserable whenever he had to go ashore. He didn't feel comfortable unless he was on a boat. I know, because one Christmas he came to our house to visit.

Usually Dr. D is fun to be with. But that Christmas visit was a nightmare.

Dr. D spent the whole time pacing through the house. He barked orders at us like a sea captain.

"Billy, sit up straight!" he yelled at me. "Sheena, swab the decks!"

He just wasn't himself.

Finally, on Christmas Eve, my dad couldn't take it anymore. He told Dr. D to shape up or ship out.

Dr. D ended up spending a good part of Christmas Day in the bathtub playing with my old toy boats. As long as he stayed in the water, he was back to normal.

I never wanted to see Dr. D stranded on land again.

"Don't worry, kids," Alexander said. "Dr. D has always found a way to get by."

I hoped Alexander was right.

I studied another strange dial, marked SONAR PROBES.

"Hey, Alexander," I said. "Will you show me how the sonar probes work?"

"Sure," said Alexander. "Just let me finish a few chores."

He walked over to the first fish tank. He scooped out a few guppies with a small net.

"Who wants to feed Biff today?"

"Not me," said Sheena. "Yuck!"

"No way!" I said as I stepped to a porthole and peered out.

I thought I heard a motor outside. So far we had seen very few other boats. Not many people passed by Ilandra.

A white boat chugged up to the side of the *Cassandra*. It was smaller but newer than our boat. A logo on the side said MARINA ZOO.

A man and a woman stood on the deck of the zoo boat. They were both neatly dressed in khaki pants and button-down shirts. The man had a short, neat haircut, and the woman's brown hair was pulled back in a ponytail. She carried a black briefcase.

The man waved to someone on the deck of the *Cassandra*. I figured he had to be waving at Dr. D.

Now Sheena and Alexander stood beside me at the porthole, watching.

"Who's that?" Sheena asked.

Alexander cleared his throat. "I'd better go see what this is about," he said.

He handed Sheena the net with the guppies in it. "Here," he said. "Feed Biff. I'll be back later."

He left the lab in a hurry.

Sheena looked at the squirming guppies in the net and made a face.

"I'm not going to stay here and watch Biff eat these poor guppies." She stuck the net in my hand and ran out of the cabin.

I didn't want to watch Biff eat the poor fish, either. But I didn't know what else to do with them.

I quickly dumped the guppies into Biff's tank. The eel's head shot forward. His teeth clamped down on a fish. The guppy disappeared. Biff grabbed for another one.

He was a fast eater.

I dropped the net on a table and walked out of the lab.

I made my way down the narrow passageway, planning to go up on deck for some air.

I wondered if Dr. D would let me do some more snorkeling this afternoon.

If he said yes, maybe I would swim toward the lagoon, see if I could find any sign of the sea monster.

Was I scared?

Yes.

But I was also determined to prove to my sister and uncle that I wasn't crazy. That I wasn't making it up.

I was passing Dr. D's office when I heard voices. I figured Dr. D and Alexander must be in there with the two people from the zoo.

I paused for just a second. I didn't mean to eavesdrop, I swear. But the man from the zoo had a loud voice, and I couldn't help but hear him.

And what he said was the most amazing thing I had ever heard in my whole entire life.

"I don't care how you do it, Dr. Deep," the man bellowed. "But I want you to find that mermaid!"

A mermaid!

Was he serious?

I couldn't believe it. Did he really want my uncle to find a real, live mermaid?

I knew Sheena would start chanting, "No such thing, no such thing." But here was a grown man, a man who worked for a zoo, talking about a mermaid. It *had* to be real!

My heart started to pound with excitement. *I might be one of the first people on earth ever to see a mermaid!* I thought.

And then I had an even better thought: *What if I was the one to find her?*

I'd be famous! I'd be on TV and everything!

William Deep, Jr., the famous sea explorer!

Well, after I heard that, I couldn't just walk away. I had to hear more.

Holding my breath, I pressed my ear to the door and listened.

"Mr. Showalter, Ms. Wickman, please understand," I heard Dr. D saying. "I'm a scientist, not a circus trainer. My work is serious. I can't waste my time looking for fairy tale creatures."

"We're quite serious, Dr. Deep," said Ms. Wickman. "There is a mermaid in these waters. And if anyone can find her, you can."

I heard Alexander ask, "What makes you think there's really a mermaid out there?"

"A fisherman from a nearby island spotted her," replied the man from the zoo. "He said he got pretty close to her — and he's sure she's real. He saw her near the reef — *this* reef, just off Ilandra."

The reef! Maybe she lives in the lagoon!

I leaned closer to the door. I didn't want to miss a word of this.

"Some of these fishermen are very superstitious, Mr. Showalter," my uncle scoffed. "For years there have been stories . . . but no real reason to believe them."

"We didn't believe the man ourselves," said the woman. "Not at first. But we asked some other fishermen in the area, and they claim to have seen the mermaid, too. And I think they're telling the truth. Their descriptions of her match, down to the smallest detail."

I could hear my uncle's desk chair creak. I

imagined him leaning forward as he asked, "And how, exactly, did they describe her?"

"They said she looked like a young girl," Mr. Showalter told him. "Except for the" — he cleared his throat — "the fish tail. She's small, delicate, with long blond hair."

"They described her tail as shiny and bright green," said the woman. "I know it sounds incredible, Dr. Deep. But when we spoke to the fishermen, we were convinced that they really saw a mermaid!"

There was a pause.

Was something missing? I pressed my ear to the door. I heard my uncle ask. "And why, exactly, do you want to capture this mermaid?"

"Obviously, a real, live mermaid would be a spectacular attraction at a zoo like ours," said the woman. "People from all over the world would flock to see her. The Marina Zoo would make millions of dollars.

"We are prepared to pay you very well for your trouble, Dr. Deep," said Mr. Showalter. "I understand you are running out of money. What if the university refuses to give you more? It would be terrible if you had to stop your important work just because of that."

"The Marina Zoo can promise you one million dollars," said the woman. "*If* you find the mermaid. I'm sure your lab could run for a long time on that much money."

A million dollars! I thought. *How could Dr. D turn down that kind of money?*

My heart pounded with excitement. I pushed against the door, straining to hear.

What would my uncle's answer be?

7

Leaning hard against the door, I heard Dr. D let out a long, low whistle. "That's quite a lot of money, Ms. Wickman," I heard him say.

There was a long pause. Then he continued. "But even if mermaids existed, I wouldn't feel right about capturing one for a zoo to put on display."

"I promise you we would take excellent care of her," replied Mr. Showalter. "Our dolphins and whales are very well cared for. The mermaid, of course, would get extra-special treatment."

"And remember, Dr. Deep," said Ms. Wickman. "If you don't find her, someone else will. And there's no guarantee that they will treat the mermaid as well as we will."

"I suppose you're right," I heard my uncle reply. "It would certainly be a big boost to my research if I found her."

"Then you'll do it?" asked Mr. Showalter eagerly.

Say yes, Dr. D! I thought. *Say yes!*

I pressed my whole body against the door.

"Yes," my uncle answered. "If there really is a mermaid, I'll find her."

Excellent! I thought.

"Very good," said Ms. Wickman.

"Excellent decision," Mr. Showalter added enthusiastically. "I knew we had come to the right man for the job."

"We'll be back in a couple of days to see how the search is going. I hope you'll have some good news by then," Ms. Wickman said.

"That's not much time," I heard Alexander remark.

"We know," Ms. Wickman replied. "But, obviously, the sooner you find her, the better."

"And please," Mr. Showalter said, *"please* keep this a secret. No one must know about the mermaid. I'm sure you can imagine what would happen if —"

CRASSSSSSSH!

I lost my balance. I fell against the door.

To my shock, it swung open — and I tumbled into the room.

I landed in a heap in the center of the cabin floor.

Dr. D, Mr. Showalter, Ms. Wickman, and Alexander all gaped at me with their mouths open. I guess they hadn't expected me to drop in.

"Uh . . . hi, everyone," I murmured. I felt my face burning and knew that I was blushing. "Nice day for a mermaid hunt."

Mr. Showalter jumped to his feet angrily. He glared at my uncle. "This was supposed to be a secret!"

Alexander strode across the room and helped me to my feet. "Don't worry about Billy," he said. He put a protective arm around me. "You can trust him."

"I'm very embarrassed," Dr. D told his visitors. "This is my nephew Billy Deep. He and his sister are visiting me for a few weeks."

"Can they keep our secret?" asked Ms. Wickman.

Dr. D turned his gaze on Alexander. Alexander nodded.

"Yes, I'm sure they can," said Dr. D. "Billy won't say anything to anyone. Right, Billy?"

He narrowed his eyes at me. I really do hate it when he does that. But this time I couldn't blame him.

I shook my head. "No. I won't tell anyone. I swear."

"Just to be on the safe side, Billy," said Dr. D, "don't mention the mermaid to Sheena. She's too young to have to keep a big secret like this."

"I promise," I replied solemnly. I raised my right hand as if swearing an oath. "I won't breathe a word to Sheena."

This was *so cool*!

I knew the biggest secret in the world — and Sheena wouldn't have a clue!

The man and woman from the zoo exchanged glances. I could see they were still worried.

Alexander said, "You really can trust Billy. He's very serious for someone his age."

You bet *I'm serious*, I thought.

I'm William Deep, Jr., world-famous mermaid catcher.

Mr. Showalter and Ms. Wickman seemed to relax a little.

"Good," said Ms. Wickman. She shook hands with Dr. D, Alexander, and me.

Mr. Showalter gathered up some papers and put them into the briefcase.

"We'll see you in a few days, then," said Ms. Wickman. "Good luck."

I won't need luck, I thought, watching them roar away on their boat a few minutes later.

I won't need luck because I have skill. And daring.

My head spun with all kinds of exciting thoughts.

Would I let Sheena be on TV with me after I single-handedly captured the mermaid?

Probably not.

That night I sneaked off the boat and slipped into the dark water. I swam noiselessly toward the lagoon.

I glanced back at the *Cassandra*. It floated quietly. All the portholes were dark.

Good, I thought. *No one is awake to notice that I'm gone. No one knows I'm out here. No one knows I'm swimming in the sea at night, all alone.*

Swimming steadily, easily, under the silvery moonlight, I made my way around the reef and into the dark lagoon.

I slowed my stroke just past the reef.

My eyes darted eagerly around the lagoon. The waves lapped gently under me. The water sparkled as if a million tiny diamonds floated on the surface.

Where was the mermaid?

I knew she was there. I knew I would find her here.

From deep below me, I heard a low rumble.

I listened hard. The sound, faint at first, grew louder.

The waves tossed as the sound became a steady roar.

It rumbled like an earthquake. An earthquake on the ocean floor.

The waves tumbled and tossed. I struggled to stay on top of them.

What was happening?

Suddenly, from the middle of the lagoon, a huge wave swelled. It rose higher, like a gigantic geyser.

Higher. Over my head. As tall as a building!

A tidal wave?

No.

The wave broke.

The dark creature pushed up underneath it.

Water slid off its grotesque body. Its single eye stared out darkly at me. Its tentacles writhed and stretched.

I screamed.

The monster blinked its muddy brown eye at me.

I tried to turn and swim away.

But it was too fast.

The tentacles whipped out — and grabbed me, tightening, tightening around my waist.

Then a slimy, cold tentacle wrapped around my neck and started to squeeze.

"I — I can't breathe!" I managed to choke out.

I tugged at the tentacle twining around my throat.

"Help me — somebody!"

I opened my eyes — and stared up at the ceiling.

I was lying in bed.

In my cabin.

The sheet was wrapped tightly around me.

I took a deep breath and waited for my heart to stop thudding. A dream.

Only a dream.

I rubbed my eyes, lifted myself, and peered out the porthole. The sun was just rising over the horizon. The sky was morning red. The water a hazy purple.

Squinting past the reef, I saw the lagoon. Perfectly still. Not a sea monster in sight.

I wiped the sweat from my forehead with my pajama sleeve.

No need to be afraid, I told myself. *It was just a dream. A bad dream.*

I shook my head, trying to forget about the sea monster.

I couldn't let it scare me. I couldn't let it stop me from finding that mermaid.

Was anyone up? Had I yelled out loud in my sleep?

I listened carefully. I could hear only the creaking of the boat, the splash of waves against its side.

The pink morning sunlight cheered me. The dark water looked inviting.

I slipped into my bathing suit and crept out of my cabin as quietly as I could. I didn't want anyone to hear me.

In the galley I saw a half-empty pot of coffee sitting on the warmer. That meant Dr. D was already up.

I tiptoed down the passageway and listened. I could hear him puttering around in the main lab.

I grabbed my snorkel, flippers, and mask and went up on deck. Nobody up there.

The coast was clear.

Silently, I climbed down the ladder, slipped into the water, and snorkeled toward the lagoon.

I know it was crazy to sneak away like that. But you can't imagine how excited I was. Even in my wildest daydreams as William Deep, Jr., undersea explorer, I never thought I would see a real, live mermaid!

As I snorkeled toward the lagoon, I tried to imagine what she would look like.

Mr. Showalter had said she looked like a young girl with long blond hair and a green fish tail.

Weird, I thought.

Half-human, half-fish.

I tried to imagine my own legs replaced by a fish tail.

I'd be the greatest swimmer on earth if I had a fish tail, I thought. *I could win the Olympics without even practicing.*

I wonder if she's pretty? I thought. *And I wonder if she can talk! I hope she can. She can tell me all kinds of secrets of the oceans.*

I wonder how she breathes underwater?

I wonder if she thinks like a human or like a fish?

So many questions.

This is going to be the greatest adventure of my life, I thought. *After I'm famous, I'll write a book about my undersea adventures. I'll call it* Courage of the Deep, *by William Deep, Jr. Maybe someone will even turn it into a movie.*

I raised my head and saw that I was nearing the reef. I concentrated on keeping away from it. I didn't want to touch that fire coral again.

I couldn't wait to explore the lagoon. I was so

excited, I forgot all about the terrifying dream I had had the night before.

I kicked my legs carefully, watching out for red coral.

I was nearly past the reef when I felt something brush my leg.

"Oh!" I cried out, and swallowed a mouthful of salty water.

Sputtering and choking, I felt something wrap around my ankle.

As it grabbed me, it scratched my ankle.

This time I knew for sure it wasn't seaweed.

Seaweed doesn't have claws!

10

Ignoring the panic that nearly froze me, I kicked and thrashed with all my strength.

"Stop it! Stop kicking me!" a voice screamed.

The mermaid?

"Hey — !" I cried out angrily as Sheena's head appeared beside me.

She pulled up her snorkeling mask. "I didn't scratch you *that* hard!" she snapped. "You don't have to go crazy!"

"What are *you* doing here?" I cried.

"What are *you* doing here?" she demanded nastily. "You know Dr. D told us not to swim here."

"Then you shouldn't be here — *should* you?" I shouted.

"I knew you were up to something, so I followed you," Sheena replied, adjusting her mask.

"I'm not up to anything," I lied. "I'm just snorkeling."

"Sure, Billy. You're just snorkeling at six-thirty in the morning exactly where you're not supposed to — *and* where you burned your foot on that fire coral yesterday. You're either up to something or you're totally crazy!" She squinted at me, waiting for a response.

What a choice! I was either up to something or crazy. Which should I admit to?

If I admitted I was up to something, I'd have to tell her about the mermaid — and I couldn't do that.

"Okay," I said with a casual shrug. "I guess I'm crazy."

"Well, big news," she muttered sarcastically. "Come on back to the boat, Billy," said Sheena. "Dr. D will be looking for us."

"You go back. I'll be there in a little while."

"Billy," said Sheena. "Dr. D is going to be very mad. He's probably ready to hop in the dinghy and search for us right now."

I was about to give up and go with her. Then, out of the corner of my eye, I saw a big splash on the other side of the reef.

The mermaid! I thought. *That's got to be her! If I don't go look for her now, I might miss her!*

I turned away from Sheena and started swimming very fast, straight for the reef.

I could hear Sheena screaming, "Billy! Come back! *Billy!*"

I thought I heard an extra note of panic in her voice, but I ignored it. *Just Sheena trying to scare me again*, I thought.

"*Billy!*" she screamed again. "*Billy!*"

I kept on swimming.

No way I was going to stop now.

But as it turned out, I should have listened to her.

Swimming fast, I raised my head, searching for a good place to swim safely over the fire coral.

I saw another splash. Across the lagoon. Near the shore.

That's *got* to be the mermaid! I thought excitedly.

I stared hard, trying to catch a glimpse of her.

I thought I saw some kind of fin.

I made my way past the reef into the deep, still waters of the lagoon. I strained to see the mermaid, but my mask had fogged.

Rats! I thought. *What a time for my mask to start leaking!*

I came up for air and pulled off the mask. I hoped I wouldn't lose sight of the mermaid because of this.

I wiped the water from my eyes and, leaving the mask wrapped around my wrist, stared toward the lagoon.

That's when I saw it. A few hundred yards away.

Not the green fish tail of a mermaid.

The fin I saw was a gray-white triangle sticking straight up in the water.

The fin of a hammerhead shark.

As I stared in horror, the fin turned in the water and then ripped toward me, moving steady and straight as a torpedo.

Where was Sheena?

Was she still behind me?

I glanced back. I could see her in the distance, splashing back to the boat.

I was forced to forget about Sheena as the gray fin swiftly moved closer.

I thrashed my arms in the water, trying to swim away.

When the shark swam right past me, I stopped thrashing.

Would it go away? Would it leave me alone?

My heart in my throat, I started swimming in the other direction, toward the reef. Away from the shark.

I kept my eyes on that fin.

It began to turn. The shark's fin streamed toward me in a wide arc.

"Ohhh." I let out a terrified groan as I realized it was circling me.

Now I didn't know which way to go. The shark

swam between me and the boat. If I could turn around and climb on to the reef, maybe I would be safe.

The huge fin slid closer.

I plunged toward the reef. I knew I had to keep distance between me and the shark.

Suddenly, the fin shot up in front of me — between me and the reef.

The shark kept circling, closing in, swimming faster and faster, making the circle smaller as he swam.

I was trapped. But I couldn't stay still. I couldn't just float there, waiting for the shark to eat me.

I had to fight. I kicked my legs in a panic as I swam toward the reef.

I was nearer to the reef now. But the shark's circles grew smaller, smaller.

I breathed in quick, shallow gasps. I couldn't think clearly. I was too terrified. The same two words echoed in my brain: *The shark. The shark.*

Over and over again. *The shark. The shark.*

The shark swam around me in a tight circle. His tail swished, sending up waves of water over me.

The shark. The shark.

I stared at the monster in wide-eyed horror. He swam so close, I could see him clearly. He was big — at least ten feet long. His head was wide and hideous, long like the head of a hammer, with an eye on each end.

I heard my voice quivering. "No . . . no . . ."

Something cold brushed my leg.

The shark. The shark.

My stomach lurched. I threw my head back and let out a howl of sheer terror.

"Aaaaaiiii!"

Pain jolted down my spine.

The shark had bumped me with its snout. My body rose out of the water, then hit the surface with a *smack*.

I froze.

The shark was hungry.

It wanted to fight.

It circled me again, then zoomed straight for me.

Its jaws opened. I saw rows and rows of sharp teeth.

I screamed out a hoarse "NO!" I thrashed, panicked. I kicked with all my strength.

The razor teeth brushed by, just missing my leg.

The reef. I had to get to the reef. It was my only chance.

I dove for the coral. The shark plunged toward me. I dodged it once more.

I grabbed the red coral. Pain shot through my hand. The fire coral.

I didn't care.

The top of the reef sat just above the surface of the water. I tried to pull myself up. My whole body stung.

I had almost made it. Soon I'd be safe.

With a mighty kick, I hoisted myself onto the reef — and was yanked back into the water.

My stomach slammed against the side of the reef. I felt a sharp stab of pain in my leg.

I tried to pull my leg away. I couldn't.

It was caught in the jaws of the shark.

My mind screamed with terror.

The shark. The shark.

It's got me!

13

My entire body burned with pain. I slipped heavily into the water.

The shark knew he had me. I had no strength left to fight.

Then something splashed nearby.

The shark released my leg and jerked toward the splash.

I had no time to catch my breath. The shark circled back. It charged at me.

The gaping jaws moved in for the kill.

I shut my eyes and let out a shrill scream of terror.

A second passed. Then another.

Nothing happened.

I heard a loud thump.

I opened my eyes.

Something had come between me and the shark, a few feet in front of me.

I stared. The water churned white. A long, shiny

green fish tail rose out of the water and splashed back down.

Another fish was fighting the shark!

The shark rolled over, then attacked. The green fish tail smacked the shark hard. The shark went under.

I couldn't see what was happening. The water rocked higher, tossing up frothy white waves.

All around me the water bubbled and churned, white with foam. Over the crash of the water, I heard shrill animal squeals.

Sharks don't squeal, do they? I thought. *What is making that sound?*

The shark surfaced, its toothy jaws gaping. It snapped them at something, once, twice. Snapping at air.

The long green fish tail rose out of the water and smacked the shark hard. A direct hit on its broad hammerhead.

The shark shut its jaws and sank below the surface.

Then I heard a loud *bump*! The water stopped churning.

A second later, the huge gray fin surfaced a few yards away, speeding off in the other direction.

The shark was swimming away!

I stared at the green fish tail as it arced over the dark swelling water.

As the waters calmed, I heard a low musical sound. It was beautiful and slightly sad. Whistling and humming at the same time.

It sounded something like a whale. But this creature was much smaller than a whale.

The green tail swung around. Then the creature lifted its head.

A head with long blond hair.

The mermaid!

Bobbing in the water, I forgot my burning pain as I gaped at her.

To my amazement, the mermaid looked just as the zoo people had said she would.

Her head and shoulders were smaller than mine, but her flashing green tail stretched out, long and powerful. Her wide sea-green eyes sparkled. Her skin gave off a pale pink glow.

I stared at her, unable to speak.

She's real! I thought. *And she's so beautiful!*

At last I found my voice. "You — you saved me," I stammered. "You saved my life. Thank you!"

She shyly lowered her eyes and cooed at me through shell-pink lips. What was she trying to say?

"What can I do in return?" I asked her. "I'll do anything I can."

She smiled and uttered that haunting low hum. She was trying to talk to me. I wished I could understand her.

She reached for my hand and examined it, frowning over the red burns from the fire coral. Her hand felt cool. She passed it over the palm of my hand, and the pain from the burns began to fade away.

"Wow!" I exclaimed. I must have sounded pretty stupid, but I didn't know what else to say. Her touch was like magic. When she held my hand, I could float without treading water. Just as she did.

Was this another dream?

I closed my eyes and opened them again.

I was still floating in the sea, staring at a blond-haired mermaid.

No. Not a dream.

She smiled again and shook her head, making those low singing sounds.

I could hardly believe that only a few minutes before, I'd been frantically fighting off a hungry shark.

I raised my head and searched the waters. The shark had vanished. The water had calmed, shimmering like gold now under the morning sunlight. And there I was, floating in the sea off a deserted island with a real mermaid.

Sheena will never believe this, I thought. *Not in a million years.*

Suddenly, the mermaid flipped her tail and disappeared under the water.

Startled, I searched around for her. She had left without a trace — not a ripple, not a bubble.

Where did she go? I wondered. *Is she gone, just like that? Will I never see her again?*

I rubbed my eyes and looked for her again. No sign of her. A few fish darted past me.

She had disappeared so instantly, I began to think I had dreamed her up after all.

Just then, I felt a tiny pinch on my foot.

"Ouch!" I yelled, quickly pulling away. I began to panic. The shark was back!

Then, behind me, I heard a small splash and a whistlelike giggle. I turned around.

The mermaid smiled mischievously at me. She snapped her fingers in a pinching motion.

"It was you!" I cried, laughing with relief. "You're worse than my little sister!"

She whistled again and slapped her tail against the surface of the water.

Suddenly, a dark shadow fell across her face. I raised my eyes to see what it was.

Too late.

A heavy net dropped over us. Startled, I thrashed my arms and legs. But that only tangled them more in the rope.

The net tightened over both of us. We were thrown together.

We struggled helplessly as the net jerked us up.

The mermaid's eyes widened and she squealed in terror.

"*EEEEEE!*" she cried.

We were being pulled up out of the water.

"*EEEEEEE!*" The mermaid's frightened wail rose like a siren, drowning out my feeble cries for help.

15

"Billy — I don't believe it!"

I gazed up through the holes in the net and recognized Dr. D and Sheena. They struggled to pull us aboard the dinghy.

Sheena stared down at me and the mermaid in amazement. Dr. D's eyes were wide, and his mouth hung open.

"You've found her, Billy!" he said. "You've actually found the mermaid!"

"Just get me out of this net!" I cried. Somehow, I didn't feel so great about capturing the mermaid anymore.

"The zoo people were right," Dr. D muttered to himself. "It's unbelievable. It's astounding. It's historic. . . ."

We landed in a heap on the floor of the dinghy. The mermaid squirmed beside me in the net, making sharp, angry clicking noises.

Dr. D watched her closely. He touched her tail.

The mermaid flapped it hard against the bottom of the boat.

"Is there any way this could be a hoax?" he wondered aloud.

"Billy — is this one of your dumb tricks?" Sheena demanded suspiciously.

"It's not a trick," I said. "Now will you get me out of this net? The ropes are digging into my skin."

They ignored me.

Sheena gently reached one finger through the net and touched the scales on the mermaid's tail. "I can't believe it," she murmured. "She's really real!"

"Of course she's real!" I cried. "We're both real, and we're both very uncomfortable!"

"Well, it's hard to believe anything *you* say," Sheena snapped. "After all, you've been talking about sea monsters ever since we got here."

"I *did* see a sea monster!" I cried.

"Quiet, kids," said Dr. D. "Let's get our discovery back to the sea lab."

He started the dinghy's motor and we roared back to the big boat.

Alexander stood on deck, waiting for us. "It's really true!" he cried excitedly. "It's really a mermaid!"

Sheena tied the dinghy to the side of the *Cassandra* while Dr. D and Alexander hoisted me and the mermaid aboard.

Dr. D opened the net and helped me out. The mermaid flopped her tail and got herself even more tangled in the net.

Alexander shook my hand. "I'm proud of you, Billy. How did you do it? This is amazing." He gave me a vigorous pat on the back. "Do you realize this is the greatest ocean find of the century? Maybe of all time?"

"Thanks," I said. "But I didn't do anything. I didn't find her — *she* found *me*."

The mermaid flopped violently on deck. Her squeals became higher-pitched, more frantic.

Alexander's face fell. "We've got to do something for her," he said urgently.

"Dr. D, you've got to let her go," I said. "She needs to be in the water."

"I'll fill the big tank with seawater, Dr. D," said Alexander. He hurried off to fill the tank.

"We can't let her go just yet, Billy," said Dr. D. "Not without examining her first." His eyes were shining with excitement. But he saw how upset I was. "We won't hurt her, Billy. She'll be all right."

His eyes dropped to my leg, and he frowned. He kneeled down to look at it.

"You're bleeding, Billy," he said. "Are you okay?"

"I'm fine," I said. "But the mermaid isn't."

He ignored me.

"How did this happen?" asked Dr. D.

"A shark grabbed my leg," I told him. "Just as he was about to clamp down, the mermaid came. She saved my life. You should have seen her fighting that shark."

Dr. D turned to the mermaid as if seeing her for the first time.

"Wow," said Sheena. "She fought off a shark? All by herself?"

The mermaid's long green tail pounded angrily on the deck of the boat.

"EEEEE! EEEEEE!" she cried shrilly. She almost sounded as if she were screaming.

"Forget about my leg," I shouted. "You've got to let the mermaid go!"

Dr. D stood up, shaking his head. "Billy, I'm a scientist. This mermaid is an extremely important discovery. If I let her go, I'd be letting down the entire scientific community. I'd be letting down the entire world!"

"You just want the million dollars," I muttered.

I knew it was cruel, but I couldn't stop myself. I hated seeing the mermaid so unhappy.

Dr. D looked hurt.

"That's not fair, Billy," he said. "I think you know me better than that."

I avoided his gaze. Lowering my head, I pretended to examine the cut on my leg. It wasn't very deep. Alexander had given me some gauze. I pressed it against the cut.

"I only want the money to continue my research," Dr. D went on. "I would never use this mermaid to get rich."

That was true. I knew Dr. D didn't care about the money for himself. All he wanted was to keep studying fish.

"Just think about it, Billy, You've found a mermaid! A creature we all thought didn't exist! We can't just let her go. We've got to find out a little bit about her," he said excitedly.

I said nothing.

"We won't hurt her, Billy. I promise."

Alexander returned. "The tank is ready, Dr. D."

"Thanks." Dr. D followed him to the other side of the boat.

I glanced at Sheena to see whose side she was on. Did she want to keep the mermaid? Or let her go?

But Sheena just stood there, watching. Her face was tense. I could tell she wasn't sure which of us was right.

But when I looked at the mermaid, I knew *I* was right.

She had finally stopped squirming and flipping her tail. Now she lay still on the deck, the net draped over her. She was breathing hard and staring out at the ocean with watery, sad eyes.

I wished I'd never tried to find her in the first place. Now all I wanted was to find some way to help her get back to her home.

Dr. D and Alexander came back. They lifted the mermaid inside the net. Alexander lifted her tail, and Dr. D held her head.

"Don't squirm, little mermaid," Dr. D said in a soothing voice. "Keep still."

The mermaid seemed to understand. She didn't flop around. But her eyes rolled wildly, and she uttered low moans.

Dr. D and Alexander carried her to the giant glass tank. It stood on the deck now, full of fresh seawater. They gently dropped her into the tank, pulling the net away as she slid into the water. Then they put a screen top over the tank and clamped it shut.

The mermaid churned the water with her tail. Then, gradually, her tail stopped moving. She grew still.

Her body slumped lifelessly to the bottom of the tank.

She didn't move or breathe.

"Noooo!" An angry cry escaped my lips. "She's dead! She's dead! We *killed* her!"

16

Sheena had moved to the other side of the tank. "Billy, look — !" she called to me.

I hurried around to her.

"The mermaid isn't dead," Sheena reported, pointing. "Look. She — she's crying or something."

My sister was right. The mermaid had slumped to the bottom of the tank and had buried her face in her hands. "Now what do we do?" I asked.

No one answered.

"We have to find a method of feeding her," my uncle said, rubbing his chin, his eyes on the tank.

"Do you think she eats like a person or a fish?" I asked.

"If only she could tell us," said Alexander. "She can't talk, can she, Billy?"

"I don't think so," I said. "She just makes sounds. Whistles and clicks and hums."

"I'll go down to the lab and get some equipment ready," said Alexander. "Maybe we can find out something about her with the sonar monitor."

"Good idea," said Dr. D thoughtfully.

Alexander hurried below.

"I think I'd better go to Santa Anita for some supplies," said Dr. D. Santa Anita was the nearest inhabited island. "I'll buy lots of different kinds of foods. We can try them out on her until we find something she likes. Would you two like anything while I'm there?"

"How about some peanut butter?" Sheena asked quickly. "There's no way Alexander can ruin a peanut butter sandwich!"

Dr. D nodded as he climbed into the dinghy. "Peanut butter it is. Anything else? Billy?"

I shook my head.

"All right," Dr. D said. "I'll be back in a few hours."

He started the motor, and the dinghy sped off toward Santa Anita.

"It's so hot," Sheena complained. "I'm going down to my cabin for a while."

"Okay," I said, my eyes on the mermaid.

It *was* hot up on deck. There was no breeze, and the white-hot noon sun beat down on my face.

But I couldn't go below deck. I couldn't leave the mermaid.

She floated behind the glass, her long tail

drooping. When she saw me, she pressed her hands and face to the glass and cooed sadly.

I waved to her through the glass.

She cooed and hummed in her low voice, trying to communicate with me. I listened, trying to understand.

"Are you hungry?" I asked her.

She stared at me blankly.

"Are you hungry?" I repeated, rubbing my stomach. "Go like this" — I nodded my head up and down — "for yes. Do this for no." I shook my head back and forth.

I stopped and waited to see what she'd do.

She nodded her head yes.

"Yes?" I said. "You *are* hungry?"

She shook her head no.

"No? You're not hungry?"

She nodded her head yes. Then she shook her head no again.

She's just copying me, I thought. *She doesn't really understand.*

I took a step back and studied her in the tank.

She's young, I thought. *She's a lot like me. That means she* must *be hungry. And she probably likes to eat what I like. Right?*

Maybe. It was worth a try.

I hurried down to the galley. I pulled open a cupboard and took out a package of chocolate chip cookies.

Okay, so it's not exactly seafood, I thought. *But who wouldn't like chocolate chip cookies?*

I grabbed a few cookies and stuffed the package back in the cupboard. Alexander came through on his way up to the deck. He was carrying some equipment in his arms.

"Getting a snack?" he asked me.

"For the mermaid," I told him. "Do you think she'll like them?"

He shrugged his broad shoulders and said, "Who knows?"

He followed me out on deck, carrying the equipment.

"What's all that stuff?" I asked him.

"I thought we could run a few tests on the mermaid to see what we can find out about her," said Alexander. "But go ahead and feed her first."

"Okay," I said. "Here goes."

I held a cookie up to the glass. The mermaid stared at it. I could see that she didn't know what it was.

"Mmmmm," I said, patting my stomach. "Yummy."

The mermaid patted her tummy, imitating me. She stared out at me blankly with those sea-green eyes.

Alexander reached up and unlatched the screen top. I handed him the cookie, and he dropped it into the tank.

The mermaid watched it falling toward her through the water. She made no attempt to grab it.

By the time it reached her, it was soggy. It fell apart in the tank.

"Yuck," I said. "Even I wouldn't eat it now."

The mermaid pushed the soggy cookie pieces away.

"Maybe Dr. D will have something she likes when he gets back," said Alexander.

"I hope so," I said.

Alexander began to set up his equipment. He put a thermometer inside the tank, and some long white plastic tubes.

"Oh, man," Alexander mumbled, shaking his head. "I forgot my notebook."

He hurried back down to the lab.

I watched the mermaid float sadly in her tank, with all the tubes coming out of it. She reminded me of the fish down in the lab.

No, I thought. *She's not a fish. She shouldn't be treated this way.*

I remembered how she had fought the shark.

She could have been killed, I thought. *Easily. But she fought the shark, anyway, just to help me.*

The mermaid cooed. Then I saw her wipe away the tears that had begun to run down her face.

She's crying again, I thought, feeling guilty and miserable. *She's pleading with me.*

I put my face against the glass, as close to hers as I could get it.

I've got to help her, I thought.

I put a finger to my lips. "*Ssshhh*," I whispered. "Stay quiet. I have to work quickly!"

I knew I was about to do something that would make Dr. D very angry.

My uncle would probably never forgive me.

But I didn't care.

I was going to do what I thought was right.

I was going to set the mermaid free.

17

My hand trembled as I reached up to unlatch the screen at the top of the tank. The tank was taller than I was. I wasn't quite sure how I'd get the mermaid out of there. But I had to find a way.

As I struggled to pull the screen off, the mermaid began to squeal, *"Eeee! EEEEEE!"*

"*Sshh!* Don't make any noise!" I warned her.

Then I felt a hand grab me by the arm. I gasped, startled.

A deep voice asked, "What are you doing?"

I turned around to see Alexander standing behind me.

I stepped away from the tank, and he let go of my arm.

"Billy, what were you doing?" he asked again.

"I was going to let her go!" I cried. "Alexander, you can't keep her in there! Look how unhappy she is!"

We both stared at the mermaid, who had slumped to the bottom of the tank again. I think she knew that I had tried to help her — and that I had been stopped.

I caught the sadness on Alexander's face. I could tell he felt sorry for her. But he had a job to do.

He turned to me and put an arm around my shoulders. "Billy, you've got to understand how important this mermaid is to your uncle," he said. "He's worked his whole life for a discovery like this. It would break his heart if you let her go."

He slowly led me away from the tank. I turned back to look at the mermaid again.

"But what about *her* heart?" I asked. "I think it's breaking her heart to be stuck in that fish tank."

Alexander sighed. "It's not ideal, I know that. But it's only temporary. Soon she'll have plenty of room to swim and play in."

Sure, I thought bitterly. *As an exhibit at the zoo, with millions of people gawking at her every day.*

Alexander removed his arm from my shoulders and rubbed his chin.

"Your uncle is a very caring man, Billy," he said. "He'll do his best to make sure the mermaid has everything she needs. But it's his duty to study her. The things he can learn from her could help people understand the oceans better — and take better care of them. That's important, right?"

"I guess so," I said.

The mermaid leaped toward it and caught it in her mouth.

She chewed, then smiled.

She liked it!

I gave her some more. She ate it.

I rubbed my stomach. "Do you like it?" I asked her. I nodded yes.

She smiled again. Then she nodded yes.

She understood me!

"What are you doing, Billy?" Alexander asked. He had come up on deck carrying two plates and a loaf of bread.

"Alexander, look!" I cried. "We communicated!"

I dropped another piece of squid into the tank. She ate it. Then she nodded yes.

"That means she likes it!" I said.

"Wow," murmured Alexander. He put down the plates and picked up his notebook. He scribbled some notes.

"Isn't that way cool?" I demanded. "I'm a scientist, too — aren't I, Alexander?"

He nodded but kept writing.

"I mean, I'm the first person on earth to communicate with a mermaid — right?" I insisted.

"If she stays with us long enough, you might be able to talk to her in sign language," he said. "Just think of the things we could learn!"

He spoke aloud as he wrote, "Likes to eat

77

squid." Then he put down his pencil and said, "Hey, wait! That's our lunch!"

Uh-oh, I thought. I hope his feelings aren't hurt.

He looked at me. He looked at the bowl. He looked at the mermaid.

Then he started laughing.

"At least *somebody* around here likes my cooking!" he exclaimed.

About an hour later, Dr. D returned with the groceries and supplies. Luckily, he had bought plenty of seafood in Santa Anita. We fed some of it to the mermaid for supper. While she ate, Dr. D checked the readings on the meters Alexander had set up in the tank.

"Interesting," Dr. D commented. "She sends out sonar signals through the water. Just as whales do."

"What does that mean?" asked Sheena.

"It means there are probably other mermaids like her," said Dr. D. "She must be trying to contact them with underwater sounds."

Poor mermaid, I thought. *She's calling to her friends. She wants to be rescued.*

I went to my cabin after supper and stared out of the little porthole.

An orange sun sank slowly into the purple horizon. A wide carpet of gold light shimmered in the rolling ocean waters. A cool breeze blew in through the porthole.

I watched the sun drop into the ocean. The sky immediately darkened, as if someone had turned off a lamp.

The mermaid is up there all alone, I thought. *She must be so frightened. A prisoner. Trapped in a fish tank in the dark.*

The door to my cabin suddenly burst open. Sheena bounded in, panting, her eyes wide.

"Sheena!" I scolded angrily. "How many times do I have to tell you to knock first?"

She ignored me. "But, Billy!" she gasped. "She's escaped! The mermaid escaped!"

18

I leaped off my bed, my heart pounding.

"She's not there!" Sheena cried. "She's not in her tank!"

I darted out of the cabin, up the hatch, and out on deck.

Part of me hoped she really had escaped to freedom. But part of me wished she could stay forever — and make my uncle the most famous scientist in the world and me the most famous nephew of a scientist!

Please let her be okay, I thought.

Up on deck, my eyes adjusted to the evening darkness. Tiny lights glowed all around the edge of the boat.

I squinted across the deck at the giant fish tank.

I ran so fast, I nearly toppled overboard. Sheena was right behind me.

"Hey!" I cried out when I saw the mermaid floating listlessly in the water, her green tail shimmering faintly in the fading light.

It took me a few seconds to realize that Sheena was laughing. "Gotcha!" she shouted gleefully. "Gotcha again, Billy!"

I groaned long and loud. Another one of Sheena's stupid tricks.

"Good one, Sheena," I said bitterly. "Very clever."

"You're just mad because I fooled you again. You're so easy to trick."

The mermaid raised her eyes to me, and a faint smile formed on her pale lips. "*Looorrrooo, looorrrooo,*" she cooed at me.

"She really is pretty," Sheena said.

The mermaid is hoping I'll let her go now, I thought. *Maybe I should. . . .*

Sheena could help me, I decided. It would be easier with two of us.

But would my sister cooperate? "Sheena —" I began.

I heard footsteps behind us. "Hey, kids." It was Dr. D. "It's almost bedtime," he called. "Ready to go below?"

"We never go to bed this early at home," Sheena whined.

"Maybe not. But I bet you don't get up so early at home, either. Do you?"

Sheena shook her head. We all stood at the tank and watched the mermaid in silence. She gave her tail a little flick and settled back down at the bottom of the tank.

"Don't worry about her," Dr. D said. "I'll check on her during the night to make sure she's all right."

The mermaid pressed her tiny hands against the glass wall of the tank. Her eyes pleaded with us, pleaded with us to set her free.

"She'll feel better once she gets to Marina Zoo," Dr. D said. "They're building a special lagoon just for her, with a reef and everything. It'll be exactly like the lagoon off Ilandra. She'll be free to swim and play. She'll feel at home."

I hope so, I thought. But I didn't feel so sure.

The *Cassandra* rocked gently on the waves that night, but I couldn't fall asleep.

I lay on my bunk, staring at the ceiling. A pale beam of moonlight fell through the porthole and across my face. I couldn't stop thinking about the mermaid.

I tried to imagine what it would feel like to be trapped in a glass tank for a whole day. It probably wouldn't be that different from being trapped in this tiny cabin, I thought, glancing around. My cabin was about as big as a closet.

It would be terrible, I thought, fiddling with the collar of my pajama top. I pushed open the porthole to let in more air.

The fish tank might not even be the worst of

it, I figured. I know Dr. D cares about the mermaid. I know he'd never hurt her.

But what will happen to her when the zoo people take her away? Who will look out for her?

Sure, they're building a fancy fake lagoon. But it won't be the same as the real lagoon. And there will be people around, staring at her all the time. They'll probably expect her to perform tricks or something; maybe jump through hoops like a trained seal.

They'll probably put her in TV commercials, too. And TV shows and movies.

She'll be a prisoner. A lonely prisoner for the rest of her life.

This is all my fault. How could I let this happen?

I have to do something, I decided. I can't let them take her.

Just then I thought I heard something — a low hum. I lay very still and listened. At first I thought it was the mermaid. But I quickly realized it was a motor.

I heard it chugging softly, from a distance. But slowly the sound moved closer.

A boat.

I sat up and peered out of the porthole. A large boat pulled quietly up beside the *Cassandra*.

Who was it? The zoo people?

In the middle of the night?

No. It wasn't the same boat. This boat was much bigger.

As I peered out the small porthole, I saw two dark figures quietly slip on board the *Cassandra*. Then two more.

My heart began to race. *Who* are *these people?* I wondered. *What are they doing?*

What should I do?

Should I sneak up and spy on them? What if they see me?

Then I heard more strange noises.

A thud. A muffled cry of pain.

It came from the deck.

The deck. Where the mermaid was trapped helplessly in her tank.

Oh, no! I thought, feeling a chill of panic. *They're hurting the mermaid!*

I charged up to the deck. Sheena ran right behind me.

Stumbling over a towrope, I grabbed the rail to steady myself. Then I darted blindly to the fish tank.

The mermaid huddled at the bottom of the tank, her arms wrapped protectively around herself.

I saw four men standing tensely near the tank. All four were dressed in black. They had black masks pulled over their faces.

One of the men held a small club in his hand.

And a body lay sprawled on the deck, facedown.

Dr. D!

Sheena screamed and ran to our uncle. She knelt beside him. "They hit him on the head!" she cried. "They knocked him out!"

I gasped. "Who are you?" I demanded. "What are you doing on our boat?"

The four men ignored me.

Two of them unfolded a heavy rope net and spread it over the fish tank. Then they let it fall into the tank, draping it over the mermaid.

"Stop it!" I yelled. "What are you doing?"

"Be quiet, kid," the man with the club muttered. He raised the club menacingly.

I watched helplessly as they tightened the net around the mermaid.

They were kidnapping her!

"Eeeee! EEEEEeeee!" she squealed in terror and started to thrash her arms, struggling to free herself from the heavy net.

"Stop it! Leave her alone!" I cried.

One of the men gave a low laugh. The other three still ignored me.

Sheena was bent over Dr. D, frantically trying to wake him up. I ran to the hatch and shouted down into the cabin, "Alexander! Alexander! Help!"

Alexander was big and strong — maybe strong enough to stop these men.

I ran back to the tank. The mermaid was trapped in the net. All four men worked to lift her out of the tank. She squirmed and fought with all her strength.

"EEEEEE!" she screamed. The high-pitched squeal hurt my ears.

"Can't you get her to shut up?" one of the men cried angrily.

"Just load her on board," the one with the club replied sharply.

"Stop!" I yelled. "You can't do that!"

Then I totally lost it.

Without thinking, I dove toward the four of them. I don't know what I planned to do. I just knew I had to stop them.

One of them pushed me away easily with one hand. "Stay away — or you'll get hurt," he muttered.

"Let her go! Let the mermaid go!" I cried frantically.

"Forget about the mermaid," said the man. "You'll never see her again."

I grabbed the rail. My heart was pounding in my chest. I gasped for breath.

I couldn't stand the mermaid's terrified screams.

I couldn't let them take her — not without a fight.

She had saved my life once. Now it was my turn to save hers.

But what could I do?

They had lifted the mermaid out of the tank. Three men held her in the net.

She squirmed and thrashed like crazy, splashing water all over the deck.

I'll tackle them, I thought. I'll knock them over. Then I'll push the mermaid into the ocean and she can swim away to safety.

Lowering my head like a football player, I took a deep breath and ran right at them.

20

"Billy — stop!" Sheena screamed.

I crashed into one of the men holding the net, butting him hard in the stomach with my head.

To my dismay, the man hardly moved.

He grabbed me with his free hand, lifted me up off the deck, and heaved me into the fish tank.

I splashed into the warm water and came up, choking and sputtering.

Through the glass, I watched the men toss the mermaid aboard their boat. They were getting away!

I tried to scramble out of the tank, but it was too tall. I kept slipping down the wet glass, unable to reach the top.

I knew there was only one person who could stop the masked men now. Alexander.

Where was he? Hadn't he heard all the noise?

"ALEXANDER!" I shouted as loud as I could. But my voice was muffled by the glass walls of the tank.

Then, finally, he appeared on the deck. I saw his big blond head and muscular body moving toward me. At last!

"Alexander!" I cried, scrambling to stay afloat in the tank. "Stop them!"

I could hear the motor of the other boat begin to rumble. One by one, the masked men lowered themselves off our boat.

Three of them had left the *Cassandra*. Only one remained on deck.

Through the glass I watched Alexander run up to him and grab his shoulder.

Yes! I thought. *Get him, Alexander! Get him!*

I'd never seen Alexander hit anyone before. But I knew he could do it if he had to.

But Alexander didn't hit the masked man. Instead, he asked, "Is the mermaid safely on board?"

The masked man nodded.

"Good," Alexander replied. "And have you got the money for me?"

"Got it."

"All right," Alexander murmured. "Let's get out of here!"

I nearly choked on a mouthful of water.

I just couldn't *believe* that Alexander was working with the masked men. He had seemed like such a good guy.

But I knew now that he had arranged the whole thing. He had to be the one who had told them the mermaid was on board our boat.

"Alexander," I cried, "how could you?"

He stared at me through the glass. "Hey, Billy, it's just business," he said with a shrug. "The zoo was going to pay a million dollars for the mermaid. But my new bosses will pay *twenty* million!" A thin smile crossed his face. "You know arithmetic, Billy. Which would you choose?"

"You rat!" I shouted. I wanted to punch him. I struggled to get out of the tank. All I managed to do was splash a lot and get water up my nose.

Alexander followed the masked man to his boat. I pounded helplessly on the glass tank.

Then I saw Sheena stand up. Lowering my gaze to the deck, I saw that Dr. D was moving.

Alexander didn't seem to notice. He stepped over Dr. D's body. He didn't even care that Dr. D could have been hurt badly.

I watched my uncle reach up and grab Alexander by the ankle.

"Whoa!" Alexander tripped and fell hard onto his elbows and his knees.

Sheena screamed and backed up to the rail.

Maybe there's still hope, I thought, my heart beating faster. Maybe they won't get away after all.

Alexander sat up, dazed, rubbing one elbow.

"Get them!" he shouted down to the masked men.

Two of the men climbed back aboard the *Cassandra* and grabbed Dr. D. Sheena ran at them, flailing at them with her puny little fists.

Of course that didn't do any good. The third masked man grabbed her arms and pinned them behind her back.

"Kick him, Sheena!" I yelled through the glass.

She tried to kick the man who held her, but he just tightened his grip. She couldn't move.

"Let them go!" I screamed desperately.

"What should we do with them?" asked one of the men.

"Whatever you do, do it quickly," said Alexander. "We've got to get out of here."

The man who held Sheena glanced in at me. I was frantically treading water, trying to stay above the surface.

"They might call the island police or the Coast Guard," he said, frowning. "We'd better kill them."

"Throw them all in the tank!" suggested one of his partners.

22

"Alexander!" Dr. D shouted. "I know you're not a cruel man. Don't let them do this."

Alexander avoided my uncle's hard stare. "Sorry, Dr. D," he muttered. "I can't stop them. If I try to, they'll kill me, too."

Without another word, he lowered himself onto the other boat.

What a creep, I thought angrily.

Two of the masked men lifted Dr. D up high and dropped him into the tank. He landed beside me with a splash.

"Are you okay?" I asked him.

He rubbed the back of his head and nodded.

Sheena was next. They tossed her in easily. She flew through the air, flailing her arms and legs. Then she plopped into the water.

The men replaced the screen lid. They clamped it shut.

I stared out at them, realizing in horror that we had no way to escape.

The water in the tank was about six feet deep. We all kicked and paddled, trying to stay above the surface. There was barely enough room for the three of us.

"All right," said one of the men. "Let's go."

"Wait!" Dr. D shouted. "You can't just leave us here!"

The three men exchanged glances. "You're right. We can't," said one.

They stepped toward us.

So they aren't heartless monsters after all, I thought. They weren't going to leave us.

But what were they going to do?

The first man signaled the other two. They raised their hands to one side of the tank.

"One, two, three —" the first man called out.

On three, they pushed the tank over the side of the deck.

We were thrown together. Then our bodies slammed against the side of the tank as it dropped into the ocean.

Ocean water seeped into the tank.

"The tank — it's sinking!" cried Dr. D.

We watched the kidnappers' boat as it roared away. Our tank rocked in its wake. Then it started to sink.

"We're going under!" Sheena screamed. "We're going to drown!"

All three of us desperately pushed against the screen. I beat my fists against it. Dr. D tried to get his shoulder against it.

But the tank tilted in the water, and we were all tossed back.

The screen was made of heavy steel mesh and clamped onto the top of the tank. We couldn't reach the clamps from inside, so we had to try to break through it.

We pushed with all our strength. It wouldn't budge.

The tank slowly sank deeper below the surface of the dark, rolling water. The moon disappeared behind a blanket of clouds, leaving us in total darkness.

We had only a minute or two before the tank dropped completely below the surface.

Sheena started to cry. "I'm so afraid!" she shrieked. "I'm so afraid!"

Dr. D pounded his fists against the glass tank wall, trying to break through.

I ran my hands all along the top of the tank, looking for a weak spot in the screen.

Then I hit something.

A tiny latch.

"Look!" I cried, pointing to the latch.

I fumbled with it, trying to open it. "It's stuck!"

"Let me try." Dr. D tore at the latch with his fingers. "It's jammed shut," he said.

Sheena took a red barrette from her hair. "Maybe we can loosen it with this," she said.

Dr. D took the barrette and scraped hard around the latch.

"It's working!" he said.

Maybe there's hope, I thought. *Maybe we'll get out of here!*

Dr. D stopped scraping and tugged at the latch.

It moved!

It opened!

"We're free!" cried Sheena.

We all pushed at the screen. We pushed again.

"Come on, kids, push harder," urged Dr. D.

We pushed again. The screen didn't move. The latch hadn't opened it after all. Two other latches held the screen in place.

Two latches we couldn't reach.

We all grew silent. The only sounds now were Sheena's soft, frightened sobs and the steady wash of the waves.

The water had risen nearly to the top of the tank. Soon it would come rushing in on us.

Suddenly, the ocean darkened. The waters grew choppy, and the tank rocked a little faster.

"What's that noise?" Sheena asked.

I listened.

Through the churning of the water, I heard a strange sound. It was very faint, as if coming from far away.

A shrill, high-pitched whistle.

"It sounds like a siren," Dr. D murmured. "Lots of sirens."

The eerie wails rose and fell over the water.

Louder. Closer.

The sound — as shrill as the screech of metal — surrounded us.

Suddenly, dark, shadowy forms swirled around the tank.

We pressed our faces to the glass.

"That sound. I've never heard anything like it. What can it be?" asked Dr. D.

"It — it's coming from all around!" I stammered.

The dark water tossed, churned by the shadowy forms. I peered through the foam, straining to see.

Suddenly, out of the murky water, a face appeared. It pressed itself against the glass, right in front of my face!

I gasped and pulled back.

Then I saw more faces. We were surrounded by small, girlish faces. Their wide eyes peered in at us menacingly.

"Mermaids!" I shrieked.

"Dozens of them!" Dr. D murmured in hushed amazement.

They churned the water with their long tails.

Their hair, dark tangles in the black water, floated around their faces. The tank rocked harder and harder.

"What do they want?" cried Sheena, her voice shrill and trembling.

"They look angry," Dr. D whispered.

I stared out at the mermaids, swirling around us like ghosts. They reached out their hands and began clutching at the tank. They smacked their tails on the water. The dark waters tossed and churned.

Suddenly, I knew. I knew what they wanted.

"Revenge," I murmured. "They've come for revenge. We took their friend. And now they're going to pay us back."

Shadowy hands pressed against the glass.

"They're pulling us under!" Dr. D cried.

I gasped in terror, staring out at the hands, black outlines against the glass.

Then, suddenly, the tank began to rise. Up out of the water, higher and higher.

"Huh? What's happening?" asked Sheena.

"They — they're pushing us back up!" I cried happily.

"The mermaids aren't taking revenge — they're saving us!" Dr. D exclaimed.

The tank brushed up against the *Cassandra*. I could see the mermaids' tiny hands working above us.

The clamps popped open. The screen was pulled off.

With a happy groan, Dr. D boosted Sheena up. She scrambled on board the boat.

Then I climbed aboard, and we both helped pull Dr. D out of the tank.

We were drenched, shivering from the cold. But we were safe.

The mermaids swarmed around the boat, their pale eyes peering up at us.

"Thank you," Dr. D called down to them. "Thank you for saving our lives."

I realized this was the second time a mermaid had saved my life. I owed them more than ever now.

"We've got to get the kidnapped mermaid back," I said. "Who knows what Alexander and those creeps will do to her!"

"Yeah," cried Sheena. "Look what they tried to do to us!"

"I wish we could rescue her," Dr. D murmured, shaking his head. "But I don't see how we can. How will we find the kidnappers' boat in the dark? They're long gone by now."

But I knew there had to be a way. I leaned over the rail, peering down at the mermaids floating beside us, chattering and cooing in the moonlight.

"Help us!" I pleaded with them. "We want to find your friend. Please — can you take us to her?"

I held my breath and waited. Would the mermaids understand me? Would they be able to help us — somehow?

The mermaids chattered and whistled to one another. Then one of them — a dark-haired mermaid with an extra-long tail — moved to the head of the group.

She began whistling and clicking to the other mermaids. She seemed to be giving orders.

The three of us stared in amazement as the mermaids began to form a long line, one mermaid after the other, stretching far out to sea.

"Do you think they're going to lead us to the kidnappers?" I asked.

"Maybe," Dr. D replied thoughtfully. "But how will the mermaids find the boat?" He rubbed his chin. "I know. I'll bet they'll use their sonar. I wish I had time to really listen to those sounds they're making —"

"Look, Dr. D!" Sheena interrupted. "The mermaids are swimming away!"

We watched the dark figures slide away through the rolling black waters.

"Quick!" I cried. "We've got to follow them."

"Too dangerous," Dr. D replied, sighing. "We can't fight Alexander and four big masked men by ourselves!"

He paced back and forth on the narrow deck. "We should call the island police," he said finally. "But what would we say? That we're chasing after a kidnapped mermaid? No one would believe us."

"Dr. D, we have to follow them. Please!" I pleaded. "The mermaids are swimming out of sight!"

He stared at me for a long moment. "Okay. Let's get going," he said finally.

I hurried to the stern to untie the dinghy. Dr. D dropped it into the water and jumped in. Sheena and I followed. Dr. D started the motor — and we raced after the shimmering line of mermaids.

The mermaids glided so quickly through the rolling waters, it was hard for the small boat to keep up with them.

About fifteen or twenty minutes later, we found ourselves in a small deserted cove. The moon drifted out of the clouds. It cast pale light on a dark boat anchored near the shore.

Dr. D cut the motor so the kidnappers wouldn't hear us approaching.

"They must be asleep," he whispered.

"How can Alexander sleep after what he did to us?" said Sheena. "He left us to drown!"

"Money can make people do terrible things," Dr. D replied sadly. "But it's good they think we're dead. They won't be expecting us."

"But where's the mermaid?" I whispered, staring at the dark boat, bobbing gently under the misty moonlight.

We drifted silently toward the darkened boat.

Well, we've found the kidnappers, I thought, holding on to the side of the dinghy as we drew near.

There's just one problem.

What do we do next?

25

The air became very still. The kidnappers' boat sat gently on the calm, glassy waters of the cove.

"What happened to all the mermaids?" Sheena whispered.

I shrugged. There was no sign of them. I imagined them swimming way down below the surface, hiding.

Suddenly, at the side of the kidnappers' boat, I saw ripples in the water.

Slowly, silently, our dinghy glided toward the boat. I stared at the ripples, trying to see what was making them. Then I saw a flash of blond hair in the moonlight.

"The mermaid!" I whispered. "There she is!"

She was floating in the water, tied to the back of the kidnappers' boat.

"They must not have a tank to keep her in," Dr. D whispered excitedly. "Lucky for us."

Suddenly, we saw other figures rippling the

water. Mermaids arched up, circling the captured mermaid. I saw tail fins raised like giant fans. I saw hands reach around the mermaid, hands tugging at the rope that held her.

The waters tossed quietly as the figures worked.

"The mermaids are setting her free," I whispered.

"What are we going to do?" Sheena asked.

"We'll just make sure she gets away safely," Dr. D replied. "Then we'll slip away. The kidnappers will never know we were here."

We watched the mermaids struggle with the rope as our dinghy washed up against the kidnappers' boat.

"Come on, mermaids!" Sheena urged under her breath. "Hurry!"

"Maybe they need some help," I said.

Dr. D began to steer toward the mermaids.

I gasped as a light flared on the kidnappers' boat. A match set flame to a torch.

An angry voice boomed, "What do you think you're doing?"

I ducked away as the flaming torch was thrust in my face.

Behind the torch, I could see the kidnapper glaring down at me. He had quickly pulled on his black mask. It covered only the top of his face.

I heard a clambering sound, cries of surprise. Alexander and the other three kidnappers appeared on the deck.

"How did you get here?" demanded the man with the torch. "Why aren't you dead?"

"We've come for the mermaid," Dr. D called up to him. "You can't keep her here!"

The torch swung past my head. I stood up in the dinghy and took a swipe at it, trying to knock it into the water.

"Billy, no!" cried Dr. D.

The kidnapper pulled the torch away. I fell forward in the dinghy, toppling over on Sheena.

"Give us back the mermaid!" Dr. D demanded.

"Finders, keepers," the kidnapper muttered. "You've made a long trip for nothing. And now look — your boat is on fire."

He lowered the torch to the dinghy and set it aflame.

27

The flames flared up, bright orange and yellow against the blue-black sky. They spread quickly across the front of the dinghy.

Sheena uttered a terrified scream and tried to back away from the flames.

In a panic, she started to leap into the water — but Dr. D pulled her back. "Don't leave the boat! You'll drown!"

The fire crackled. The bright flames shot higher.

Dr. D grabbed a yellow life jacket from the bottom of the dinghy and started frantically beating out the fire.

"Billy — get a life jacket!" he yelled. "Sheena — find the bucket. Throw water on the flames — hurry!"

I found a life jacket and beat at the flames. Sheena dumped seawater on them as fast as she could.

Over the crackling flames, I heard Alexander shout, "Get the mermaid aboard. Let's get out of here!"

"Dr. D!" I cried. "They're getting away!"

Then I heard the kidnappers yelling. "The mermaid! Where's the mermaid?"

I turned to the side of the boat. The mermaid was gone. Her friends had freed her.

One of the kidnappers reached down from his boat and grabbed me. "What did you do with the mermaid?" he demanded.

"Let him go!" shouted Dr. D.

I tried to squirm away from the kidnapper. He held me tight. Then I saw another kidnapper swing a club at Dr. D's head.

Dr. D dodged the club. The kidnapper tried to hit him in the stomach. Dr. D dodged again.

I kicked and squirmed. Sheena tugged at the kidnapper's hands, trying to help me escape.

The third kidnapper picked her up by the wrists and threw her to the floor of the dinghy.

"Let go of the kids!" pleaded Dr. D. "Alexander! Help us!"

Alexander didn't move from his spot on the deck. He stood with his brawny arms crossed in front of him, calmly watching the fight.

The flames had nearly been quenched, but they suddenly flared up again.

"Sheena — the fire!" I cried. "Put out the fire!"

She grabbed the bucket and poured seawater everywhere.

One of the kidnappers kicked the bucket from her hands. It landed in the water with a splash.

Sheena picked up a life jacket and beat the last of the flames out.

"Drop down into their boat and toss them in the water!" I heard a kidnapper shout up above.

A man started to lower himself into our dinghy. But suddenly he lurched forward, his arms flailing. He let out a cry of surprise as his boat began to rock violently to the left. It looked as if it had been slammed by a huge wave.

The kidnappers cried out as their boat began to rock back and forth. Slowly at first. Then violently. Gripping the sides of the dinghy, I watched them clinging to the rail, screaming in confusion and surprise.

Dr. D slowly stood up, trying to see what was happening.

The boat tossed violently, as if bucking tall waves.

The mermaids. I could see them now.

They had surrounded the kidnappers' ship and were rocking it hard.

Hard. Harder. The kidnappers hung on helplessly.

"Mission accomplished!" Dr. D cried happily. He started up the motor and we roared off.

Turning back, I could see the boat tilting and rocking in the water. And I could see our mermaid swimming free, behind the other mermaids in the shimmering waves.

"She got away!" I cried. "She's free!"

"I hope she'll be all right," said Sheena.

"We'll look for her tomorrow," said Dr. D as he steered us back to the sea lab. "We know where to find her now."

Sheena glanced at me. I glanced back.

Oh, no, I thought. *After all this, it can't be true.*

Is Dr. D going to catch the mermaid again — and give her to the zoo?

Sheena and I met in the galley the next morning. Since Alexander was gone, we had to fix our own breakfasts.

"Do you think the mermaid went back to the lagoon?" asked Sheena.

"Probably," I replied. "That's where she lives."

She spooned some cereal into her mouth and chewed with a thoughtful look on her face.

"Sheena," I said, "if someone gave you a million dollars, would you show them where the mermaid lives?"

"No," Sheena replied. "Not if they wanted to capture her."

"Me, neither," I said. "That's what I don't get. Dr. D is a great guy. I just can't believe he'd —"

I stopped. I heard a noise. The sound of a motor.

Sheena listened. She heard it, too.

We dropped our spoons and ran up on deck.

Dr. D was standing on the deck, staring out to sea.

A boat was approaching. A white boat with MARINA ZOO stenciled on the side in large letters.

"The zoo people!" I said to Sheena. "They're here!"

What would our uncle do? I wondered with growing dread. Would he tell them where the mermaid was? Would he accept the million dollars?

Sheena and I ducked behind the cockpit. We watched the Marina Zoo boat tie up beside the *Cassandra*. I recognized Mr. Showalter and Ms. Wickman.

Mr. Showalter tossed a rope to Dr. D. Ms. Wickman jumped aboard.

The zoo people smiled and shook Dr. D's hand. He nodded at them solemnly.

"We had word from the fishermen on Santa Anita that you found the mermaid," Mr. Showalter said. "We're ready to take her with us now."

Ms. Wickman opened her briefcase and pulled out a slender envelope. "Here is a check for one million dollars, Dr. Deep," she said, smiling.

"We've made it out to you and the *Cassandra* Research Lab."

She held out the check to my uncle.

I peered out from behind the cockpit. *Please don't take it, Dr. D*, I pleaded silently. *Please don't take the check*.

"Thank you very much," my uncle said. He reached out a hand and took the check from her.

"A million dollars means a great deal to me and my work," Dr. D said. "Your zoo has been very generous. That's why I'm sorry I have to do this."

He raised the envelope and tore it in half.

The two zoo people gasped in surprise.

"I can't take the money," Dr. D said.

"Just what are you saying, Dr. Deep?" Mr. Showalter demanded.

"You sent me on a wild goose chase," my uncle replied. "I have searched these waters thoroughly ever since you left. With my equipment, I searched every inch of the lagoon and all the surrounding waters. I am now more convinced than ever before that mermaids do not exist."

Yaaaay! I screamed to myself. I wanted to jump up and down and cheer my head off — but I stayed hidden with Sheena behind the cockpit.

"But what about the fishermen's stories?" Ms. Wickman protested.

"The local fishermen have told mermaid stories for years," Dr. D told her. "I think they believe they've really seen mermaids rising through the mist on foggy days. But what they have seen are only fish, or dolphins, or manatees, or even swimmers. Because mermaids don't exist. They're fantasy creatures."

Mr. Showalter and Ms. Wickman both sighed in disappointment.

"Are you sure about this?" Mr. Showalter asked.

"Completely sure," my uncle replied firmly. "My equipment is very sensitive. It can pick up the tiniest minnow."

"We respect your opinion, Dr. Deep," Mr. Showalter said with some sadness. "You're the leading expert on exotic sea creatures. That's why we came to you in the first place."

"Thank you," said Dr. D. "Then I hope you'll take my advice and drop your hunt for a mermaid."

"I guess we'll have to," said Ms. Wickman. "Thank you for trying, Dr. Deep."

They all shook hands. Then the zoo people got back on their boat and motored away.

The coast was clear. Sheena and I came bursting out of our hiding place.

"Dr. D!" cried Sheena, throwing her arms around him. "You're the greatest!"

A wide grin spread over Dr. D's face. "Thanks, guys," he said. "From now on, none of us will say anything to anyone about mermaids. Is it a deal?"

"It's a deal," Sheena instantly agreed.

"Deal," I said. We all shook hands.

The mermaid was our secret.

I swore I'd never mention the mermaid to anyone. But I wanted to see her one last time. I wanted to say good-bye.

After lunch, Sheena and Dr. D went to their cabins to nap. We had been up for most of the night, after all. I pretended to take a nap, too.

But once they were asleep, I sneaked out of my cabin and slipped into the bright blue water.

I swam over to the lagoon to search for the mermaid.

The sun was high in a pale blue sky. It glowed down on the still lagoon waters, making them glitter as if covered in gold.

Mermaid? Where are you? I wondered.

I was just past the reef when I felt a playful tug on my leg.

Sheena? I thought. Had she followed me *again*?

I spun around to catch her.

No one there.

Seaweed, probably, I thought. I kept swimming.

A few seconds later, I felt the tug again. Harder this time.

Hey — it must be the mermaid! I told myself.

I turned once again to search for her.

The water rippled.

"Mermaid?" I called

A head popped out of the water.

A gigantic, slimy, dark green head.

With one enormous eye.

And a mouthful of jagged teeth.

"The sea monster!" I shrieked. "The sea monster!"

Would they believe me this time?

BEHIND THE SCREAMS

DEEP TROUBLE

CONTENTS

Bonus material
written and compiled
by Matthew D. Payne

About the Author

R.L. Stine's books are read all over the world. So far, his books have sold more than 300 million copies, making him one of the most popular children's authors in history. Besides Goosebumps, R.L. Stine has written the teen series Fear Street and the funny series Rotten School, as well as the Mostly Ghostly series, The Nightmare Room series, and the two-book thriller *Dangerous Girls*. R.L. Stine lives in New York with his wife, Jane, and Minnie, his King Charles spaniel. You can learn more about him at www.RLStine.com.

Q & A with R.L. Stine

What's the scariest moment you've ever experienced in the water?

R.L. Stine (RLS): *I'm pretty much always fearful in the water. But one Caribbean snorkeling trip was really scary: a big fish came up and bit me! I was terrified. But later, when a friend showed me a picture he took of the "huge biting fish" I saw it was about the size of a goldfish!*

Billy Deep has a wild imagination and a thirst for adventure. Were you a lot like Billy when you were a kid?

RLS: *Not at all. I never left my room. I was always writing stories and drawing comics. I made up a superhero called Super Stooge. He wasn't smart enough to have any scary adventures!*

What advice do you have for readers who hope to write their own books some day?

RLS: *My advice is to read as much as you can, and to try and write something, anything, every day. Think of it this way — when you write, you are a writer!*

If you had become an undersea explorer instead of an author, which creatures would you pursue?

RLS: *Tuna fish — on toast! Actually, I've always been fascinated by stingrays. I saw a lot of them on a trip I took to Australia.*

In Goosebumps HorrorLand #2: *Creep from the Deep,* Billy and Sheena face off against some very "spirited" villains! Is the worst behind them? Or will future books bring even deeper trouble?

RLS: Creep from the Deep *is a day at the beach compared to what's waiting for the brother and sister in HorrorLand. Here's one hint: Nobody will be able to recognize Sheena after her adventure in HorrorLand.*

To hear about the creepiest toy R.L. Stine ever played with, pick up the new collector's edition of **MONSTER BLOOD** and look in the back of the book.

There's Something Fishy About Mermaids

Mermaids certainly lent a helping hand (and fin) to Billy, Sheena, and Dr. D. But you should always approach these mythical creatures with caution. Mermaids can be found all around the world, and some aren't that friendly!

Many European cultures tell stories of mermaids that lure victims with their beauty and magical singing, only to eat them or hold them prisoner underwater! In Japan, seafarers tell tales of horrific mermaids that are nearly all-fish: Only their head is human. These creepy, eel-like creatures are thought to be the messengers of a serpent princess.

Friendlier mermaids come up on land to visit humans. Irish mermaids, while walking on their tails, must have endless patience to slowly shuffle from place to place when visiting land! In ancient Egypt, mermaids were thought to have webbed feet. It made quick visits on land a whole lot easier.

AM I PART MERMAID?

Many families in Ireland and France insist they have mermaid ancestors. If you've ever felt like a fish out of water, maybe you're part mermaid, too!

MERMAID AHOY!

Famous explorers Christopher Columbus and Henry Hudson sighted mermaids on their voyages.

SINK YOUR TEETH INTO SOME SHARK FACTS!

The whale shark is the largest shark and the largest fish in the ocean. Scientists think whale sharks can grow up to 65 feet long — the length of 1 ½ school buses.

At 10 inches long, the spined pygmy shark is the smallest shark in the ocean. Despite its small size, it packs a BIG surprise: The spined pygmy shark glows in the dark.

Sharks can detect the invisible electric fields emitted by all living things. This means that even fish hiding under the sand can end up on a lunch menu!

Certain sharks can smell a single drop of blood from almost 100 yards away — the length of a football field.

Sharks keep the tooth fairy busy. They constantly lose and regrow their teeth. Some sharks lose up to 30,000 teeth in a lifetime.

Scientists are not sure if sharks actually sleep. Sharks at "rest" will still follow divers with their eyes.

Don't start a staring contest with a shark! Although they have eyelids, sharks don't blink.

Sharks have been on earth for around 400 million years. They were here before the dinosaurs!

TALES OF HORROR: WHEN SHARKS ATTACK

1916 During one horrific summer, five people were attacked by sharks in the waters near Matewan, New Jersey — only one person survived.

1960 A shark lifted a small Australian dinghy out of the water. All three passengers held tight, and the shark swam away.

2007 A cargo ship tipped over in heavy seas off the coast of the Philippines. Some people survived the shipwreck only to be eaten by sharks, according to witnesses.

2007 A surfer in California is lucky to be alive after a shark missed his lunch and bit the surfer's board instead.

HOW TO SURVIVE A SHARK ATTACK

A person is more likely to be attacked by a pig than by a shark. However, if you ever find yourself staring down a shark, here are a few things that you can do to defend yourself:

1) Don't panic! Sharks are attracted to splashing. You even have to FEEL calm. Sharks can sense fear.

2) Poking and punching is good, but aim for the eyes and gills. The nose is too close to the mouth — your hand could quickly become an appetizer.

3) Make the shark work for his meal. Don't give up or play dead. As long as you fight, there's a chance the shark will give up and look for an easier meal.

An Undersea Adventure — Starring YOU!

Want to be like Billy Deep? Finish the following statements to make up your own undersea adventure.

I am an intrepid undersea adventurer, scouring the deep sea for . . .
> . . . treasure.
> . . . mysterious creatures.
> . . . a tasty tuna.

I am swimming . . .
> . . . into an underwater cave.
> . . . through a fire coral reef.
> . . . through a sunken pirate ship.

I am carrying . . .
> . . . an underwater camera.
> . . . a spear.
> . . . a light.

Suddenly, I run into . . .
> . . . a mermaid.
> . . . a disgusting sea creature with a huge eye and gross, slimy tentacles.
> . . . a great white shark.

What happens next? Write down anything that comes to mind and have fun crafting your tale. Remember what R.L. Stine says: "When you write, you're a writer!"

Don't miss the return of Billy and Sheena Deep in

#2 CREEP FROM THE DEEP

Turn the page for a peek at the all-new, all-terrifying thrill ride from R.L. Stine.

4

The engines roared. Dr. D turned the wheel, and the *Cassandra* edged sharply into the waves.

Sheena and I took our places on a bench against the cabin wall. The boat rocked hard, and a strong spray washed over the railing.

Soon, we were crashing over the sparkling waves. A red-orange sun floated on the horizon. I turned back and saw the tiny island of Careebo vanish, a speck of yellow on the blue water.

About an hour later, Dr. D locked the wheel. Then he led the way down to the galley for some lunch.

Normally, the *Cassandra* has a crew of three or four. But when Sheena and I visit in the summer, Dr. D likes to give them time off.

He pulled out the grilled bluefish left over from last night's dinner and some sandwich rolls, and we sat around the small white table and ate fish sandwiches and drank papaya juice.

After lunch, Dr. D pulled off his glasses and cleaned them with his napkin. "I'll tell you what we're doing," he said. "But you probably won't believe me."

He chuckled. "I'm not sure I believe it myself. But we're going to try to track down a sunken pirate ship."

My mouth dropped open. "You mean like *real* pirates?" I said.

Dr. D nodded and slid his glasses back on. "People have been searching for this ship for over two hundred years," he said. "My workers back on the mainland think they have located it using acoustic imaging and laser mapping. They just e-mailed me all the info."

Dr. D's eyes flashed. "Here's the amazing thing," he said. "If the sonar image is correct, we're actually not too far from where the ship went down."

Sheena and I nodded and waited for him to tell us more.

"The ship is called the *Scarlet Skull*," he said. "Perfect name for a pirate ship, right?"

He took a long sip of papaya juice. "According to legend, the ship sank in the late 1780s," he said. "And it took millions of dollars of jewels and gold treasure down with it."

"And we're going to find the treasure and be *billionaires*!" I cried. I jumped up and pumped my fists in the air.

Sheena grabbed me and pulled me back down. "Billy, were you *born* immature?"

"If we find the treasure, it will all go to the Careebo Dolphin Rescue Fund," Dr. D said. "I'd be thrilled to find it. But I'm a scientist — not a treasure hunter."

"This is totally cool!" I said. I was so excited, I could barely sit still.

"How did the pirate ship go down?" Sheena asked.

Dr. D scratched his head. "This is where the story gets weird," he said. "And this is what I want to investigate. The reports at the time said there were *two* pirate ships. They were sailing in view of each other. It was a calm, clear day. The ocean waves were flat and gentle. And suddenly, a swirling black cloud swept over the water. The *Scarlet Skull* sailed into the cloud — and disappeared."

"Huh? It just disappeared?" I said.

Dr. D nodded. "I *told* you it was weird. The black cloud passed, and the pirate ship had vanished. The pirates on the other ship stood staring, waiting for it to reappear. But . . . it was never seen again."

Sheena and I stared at him. Neither of us spoke.

Dr. D opened a file of papers he had brought to lunch and scanned them quickly. "The *Scarlet*

Skull belonged to a notorious captain named Long Ben One-Leg," he said. "Long Ben was very bad news."

I felt a shiver at the back of my neck. "How bad?" I asked.

"Well, some people believe that he was so evil, the sea just swallowed him up. Swallowed him and his entire ship to protect the world from his evil."

Dr. D continued to skim the papers. "Here's a story that will give you a good idea of what Captain Ben was like. It seems he kept a big tub of hungry rats on the ship. When one of his men did something to make him angry, he tossed the guy into the tub. Then he sat back and watched the rats make lunch of him."

Sheena grabbed her throat and groaned. "Ohhh, that's way sick!"

"Sometimes when he was bored," Dr. D continued, "he threw someone in the rat tub just for entertainment."

"They didn't have TV in those days, right?" I joked.

But when I pictured the hungry rats gnawing on some poor guy, I felt a little sick.

"So all the pirates drowned when the ship went down?" Sheena asked.

Dr. D nodded. "The pirates drowned. The rats drowned. And the treasure sank with them."

He set the papers on the table and squeezed

Sheena's hand. "And there's one more part to the story. A very creepy part."

He stopped as if he didn't want to tell us.

We waited, our eyes locked on his. "Tell us," I said. "Please. Tell us!"

Dr. D hesitated. I could see he was thinking hard.

"Well . . ." he said finally. "According to legend, the *Scarlet Skull* is haunted. Long Ben prowls the sunken ship — always awake, always alert — to protect the treasure."

I gasped.

But Sheena laughed. "Uncle George, you don't believe in *ghosts* — do you?"

Dr. D gazed back at her through his thick glasses. He didn't reply.

"*Do* you?" Sheena insisted. "Do you really believe in ghosts?"

"He . . . he's not a *ghost*," Dr. D muttered. "According to the legend, he's a *zombie*."

And suddenly in my mind, sounding so distant, so far away, I heard a soft, evil whisper: "*I'm waiting for you . . . I'm waiting.*"

Did Sheena and Dr. D see me shiver?

I don't think they noticed.

Of course, the whispered voice was only in my mind. My wild imagination taking off again. I was sitting there scaring MYSELF!

This is the perfect mission for the Undersea Mutant, I told myself. *Zombie pirates in a sunken treasure ship. Awesome!*

So why did my stomach suddenly feel as if I'd swallowed a huge rock?

"Tell us the truth," my sister said, pressing our uncle. "Zombies — true or false?"

That made Dr. D smile. "I'm a scientist," he said. "I study the real world. I don't believe in zombie pirates."

The *Cassandra* bounced hard on the waves. We tilted forward, then back. I gripped the edge of the table to steady myself.

I glanced out the galley porthole. In the distance, I could see islands of dark, craggy rocks and tall purple cliffs.

"I don't believe in zombies," Dr. D repeated. "But I have been *fascinated* by this mystery for years. And if we can find the ship, I can study the natural causes. I can determine what *really* made that ship go down."

Dr. D jumped up. He collected our plastic dishes and dropped them into the tiny galley sink. "Come on," he said. "I want to show you something."

He led us up to the main deck and around to the starboard side. Normally, he keeps a small dinghy tethered to the side — a little boat for going onshore on islands.

"Whoa!" I let out a startled cry. In place of the dinghy, a tiny *submarine* floated beside the *Cassandra*.

"It's my own design," Dr. D said. "Cute, huh? I call it the *Deep Diver*."

My heart was racing. Were we really going down to the bottom of the ocean in this little sub?

I leaned over the rail and studied it. It looked like a toy. Shaped like a real submarine. Bright yellow metal with a narrow hatch on top, big enough for only one person at a time.

I saw round glass portholes in front, back, and on both sides. Two big headlights in front. Twin thrusters at the back.

"The three of us should fit okay," Dr. D said. "It'll be a snug ride. My little sub won't go long distances. But it'll take us down to the sunken ship — if we find it. And it has a little speed. I can get it up to five knots if I really push it."

Another dangerous mission for the Undersea Mutant! I thought.

I imagined myself in a furious sword fight with a zombie pirate. Then I saw myself swimming away in victory, pulling a huge treasure chest brimming with jewels behind me.

NOW A MAJOR
MOTION PICTURE
JACK BLACK
Goosebumps
VILLAGE ROADSHOW PICTURES
THIS FILM IS NOT YET RATED FOR FUTURE INFO GO TO FILMRATINGS.COM
/GoosebumpsTheMovie
SCHOLASTIC
COLUMBIA PICTURES

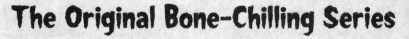

Catch the
MOST WANTED
Goosebumps® villains
UNDEAD OR ALIVE!

SCHOLASTIC
scholastic.com/goosebumps

Available in print
and eBook editions